PUZZLE QUEST

ghost hunter

Written & illustrated
by Kia Marie Hunt

Published by Collins
An imprint of HarperCollins Publishers
HarperCollins Publishers
Westerhill Road
Bishopbriggs
Glasgow G64 2QT

www.harpercollins.co.uk

HarperCollins Publishers
Macken House
39/40 Mayor Street Upper
Dublin 1, D01 C9W8, Ireland

10 9 8 7 6 5 4 3 2 1

ISBN 978-0-00-859956-0
Printed and bound in the UK using 100% renewable electricity
at CPI Group (UK) Ltd

Publisher: Michelle I'Anson
Author and illustrator: Kia Marie Hunt
Project Manager: Sarah Woods
Designer: Kevin Robbins

PUZZLE QUEST

Ghost hunter

Written and illustrated by
Kia Marie Hunt

A rather peculiar advert catches your eye in the most recent issue of Ghost Hunter Weekly Magazine...

Expert Ghost Hunter Needed!
Location: **Wight Manor**
Ghosts/Hauntings: **5+**

"For the Manor of Wight,
I seek a hunter of ghosts.
You musn't be easy to fright,
if you apply to this post.
Lead all the spirits into the light,
and you'll help this haunted host."

Request by: **Lady Wight**

How curious!

The Lady of Wight Manor is seeking an expert ghost hunter to investigate the ghosts that are haunting her big old manor house and the surrounding grounds...

Will you be the one to find the ghosts, uncover the mystery of their unfinished business and free them from the places they are bound to haunt?

Search the mysterious manor and grounds for ghosts, spirits and wisps. Be ready to solve more than 100 fun puzzles, hunting and collecting clues along the way!

Things you'll need:

* **This book**
* **A pen or pencil**
* **Your amazing brain**

That's it!

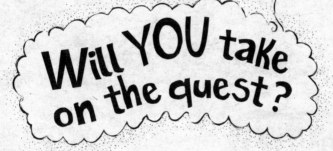

**Psssst!
Always look out for
this hand symbol:**

This means you've found a clue.

Write down all the clues you find in your Clue Logbooks
(on pages **30, 54, 78, 102** and **126!**)

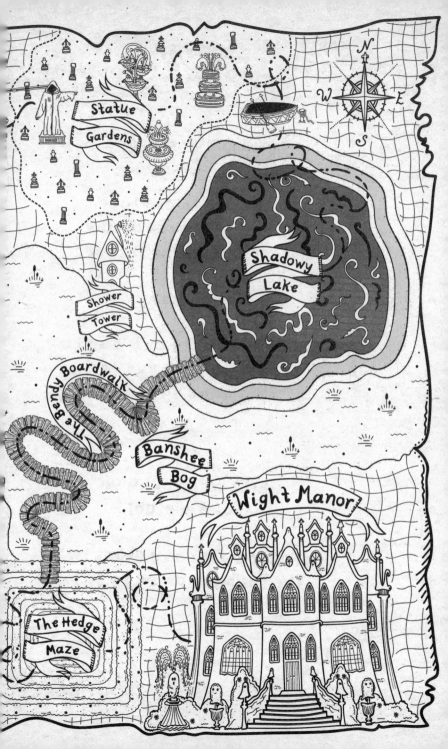

GHOST ONE

Get ready to explore the vast grounds of the mysterious Wight Manor, searching for the first ghost of many...

On your ghost hunt, don't forget to look out for this hand symbol:

which means you've found a clue!

(Record all your clues in the logbook on Page 30.)

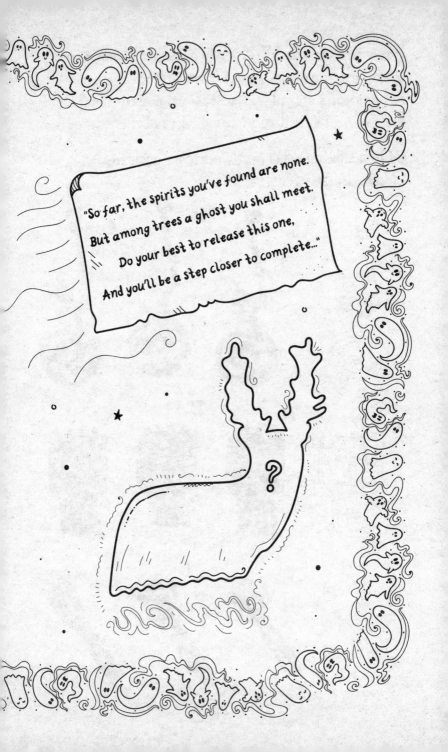

"So far, the spirits you've found are none.
But among trees a ghost you shall meet.
Do your best to release this one,
And you'll be a step closer to complete..."

For your visit to Wight Manor, you'll need to bring all your best ghost-hunting equipment. So, get your ectoplasm detectors, paranormal field meters and spirit-glow torches ready!

Which silhouette correctly matches each tool? Circle your answers.

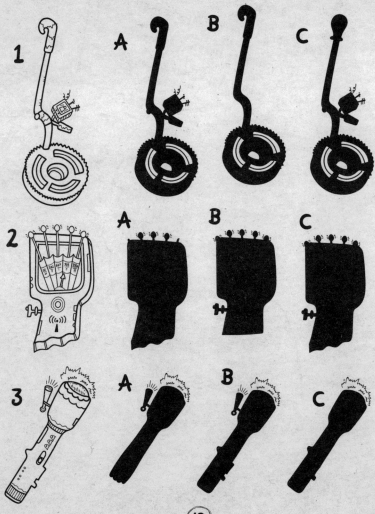

Don't forget your phantom frequency radio, spectre binoculars and whisperphone too! You never know when one of your gadgets might come in handy on a ghost hunt like this...

Odd one out: which ghost-hunting gadget does not have a matching pair? Circle your answer.

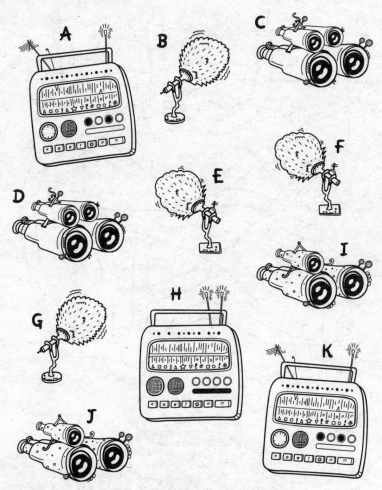

With all your tools prepared and packed, you're
ready to enter the gates to Wight Manor.

Follow the tangled paths. Which one leads
you all the way to the Manor Gates?
Write your answer in the box.

Wow, the Manor grounds are huge! Now you're inside, it's time to discover the location of the first ghost you'll be hunting...

Solve the number problem below each letter in the Key, then use the answers to fill in the gaps and reveal the location. One letter has been done for you.

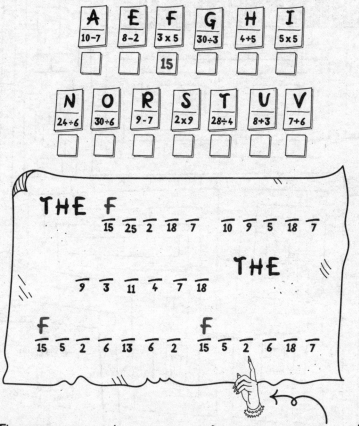

THE F _ _ _ _   _ _ _ _ _
    15 25 2 18 7   10 9 5 18 7

                    THE
      _ _ _ _ _ _
      9 3 11 4 7 18

F _ _ _ _ _ _   F _ _ _ _ _ _
15 5 2 6 13 6 2   15 5 2 6 18 7

(This symbol means this letter is your first clue, congratulations! Don't forget to write it into your Clue Logbook on page 30!)

Let the ghost hunting begin!

Can you make your way from the Manor Gates and through the maze all the way to the forest?

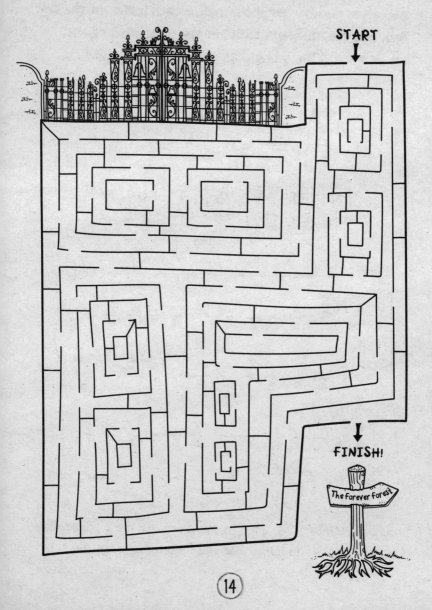

START

FINISH!

The forever forest

The trees in this forest are so old that they're known locally as the Forever Trees.

Make your way from start to finish. You can move up, down or sideways but you can't move diagonally and you must follow the trees in this order:

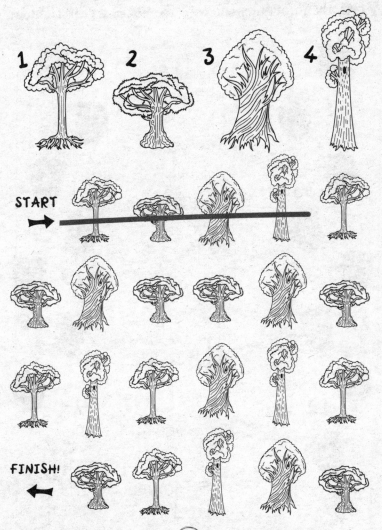

Your ectoplasm detector is beeping! When you shine your spirit-glow torch on the ground, you can see why... you've discovered ghostly animal tracks.

Follow the numbers down each set of footprints and figure out which number is next in the sequence. Write the final numbers into the boxes at the bottom.

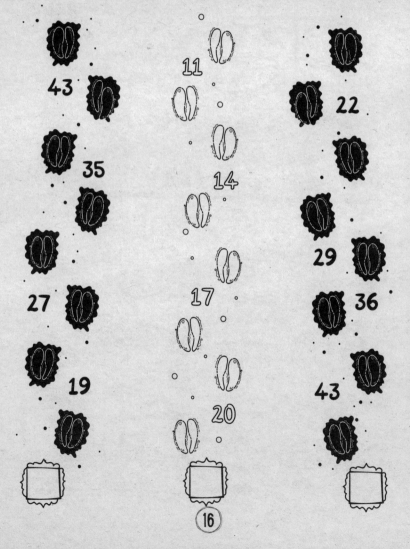

You follow the footprints as they take you deeper into the Forever Forest. Your detector is going wild! You must be getting closer...

The numbers 1, 2, 3 and 4 should be added to each row, each column and each 2x2 bold outlined box, but should only appear once in each one. The first one has been done for you.

There, in the clearing! A luminous ghost with a blue-white glow! It looks like... a ghostly deer?

Can you spot all six differences between these two pictures of the ghost?

You've found a ghost! So this Manor really is haunted. Now you need to find out all you can about this ghostly deer – let's start with their name...

Use the grid references to work out each letter, then write them onto the lines below to reveal the name of this ghost. The first letter has already been done for you.

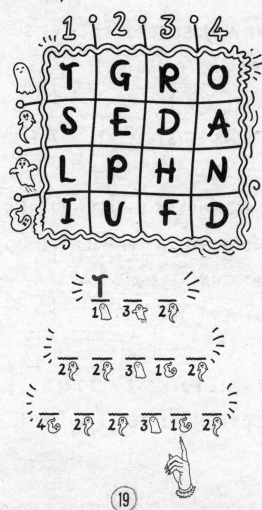

T
___ ___ ___
1   3   2

___ ___ ___ ___ ___
2   2   3   1   2

___ ___ ___ ___ ___ ___
4   2   2   3   1   2

In order to release the ghost, you need to find out why they are stuck in the Forever Forest – what is their ghostly 'unfinished business'?

Follow the tangled lines and write the letter from the circle into the space at the other end of the line to fill in the gaps and discover the ghost's 'unfinished business'...

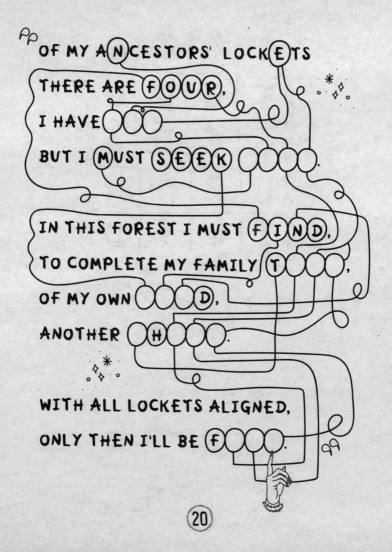

OF MY A(N)CESTORS' LOCK(E)TS
THERE ARE (F)(O)(U)(R),
I HAVE (○)(○)(○)
BUT I (M)UST (S)(E)(E)K (○)(○)(○).

IN THIS FOREST I MUST (F)(I)(N)(D),
TO COMPLETE MY FAMILY (T)(○)(○)(○),
OF MY OWN (○)(○)(○)(D),
ANOTHER (○)(H)(○)(○)(○).

WITH ALL LOCKETS ALIGNED,
ONLY THEN I'LL BE (F)(○)(○)(○).

Complete the number problems above each locket and write your answers into the circles.

Each locket should have the same answer.
The odd one out is the locket that the ghost already has — the other three still need to be found.
Which locket does the ghost have?

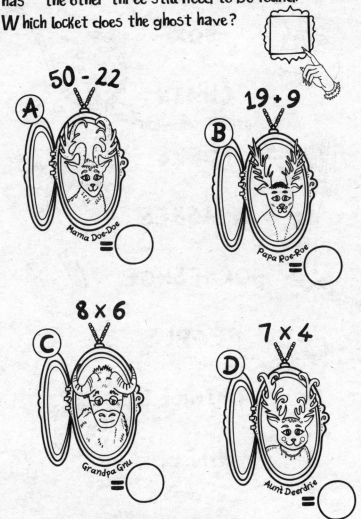

50 - 22

A

Mama Doe-Doe

=

19 + 9

B

Papa Roe-Roe

=

8 × 6

C

Grandpa Gnu

=

7 × 4

D

Aunt Deerdrie

=

Looking for lockets hidden in the Forever Forest is easier said than done. Every time you think you have found one, it turns out to be a different random object. This forest is full of weird and wonderful hidden treasures (and junk!).

BOX

CHAIN

FORKS

GLASSES

HORSESHOE

PEARLS

TRINKET

WHEEL

Can you find all eight of the found objects from the list on the opposite page in the wordsearch below?

Words may be hidden horizontally or vertically.

```
T R G Q U C H A I N M
B C L E P T F B P H S
W L A R U H B R Q E M
H E S N I O H T R F X
E A S V W R R U O O S
E N E S E S E P Z R I
L E S A R E L E S K C
K R P O B S T A E S I
E J E S T H R R R O B
R C D T C O O L O R O
T R I N K E T S A R X
```

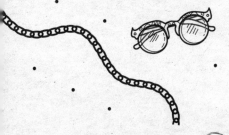

(23)

Yes! You've found Mama Doe-Doe's locket!

Scribble out every other letter from left to right. Write the letters that are left over onto the lines below to reveal the first hiding place where you found a locket. The first two letters have been scribbled out for you.

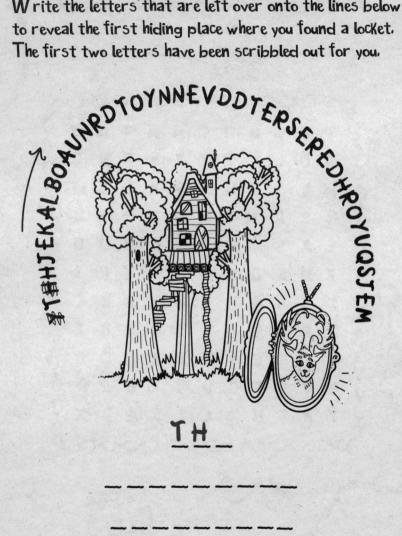

TAHJEKALBOAUNRDTOYNNEVDDTERSEREDHROYUQSJEM

T H _

_ _ _ _ _ _ _ _

_ _ _ _ _ _ _ _

Use the symbol Key to crack the code and fill in the missing letters to find out what happens next... Some letters have already been done for you.

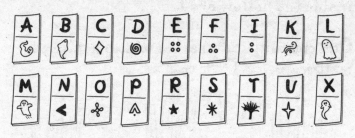

YOU
_ _ _ _

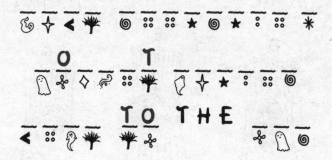

_ _ _ _ _ _ _ _ _ _ _ _ _ _ '

_ O _ _ _ _   _ T _ _ _ _

TO THE
_ _ _ _ _ _   _ _ _

_ _ _ _ _ .

And finally, after what feels like hours of searching in this old and eerie forest, you find the last locket (Papa Roe-Roe's) hidden away inside the hollow of a tree...

Odd one out: which tree hollow does not have a matching pair? Circle your answer.

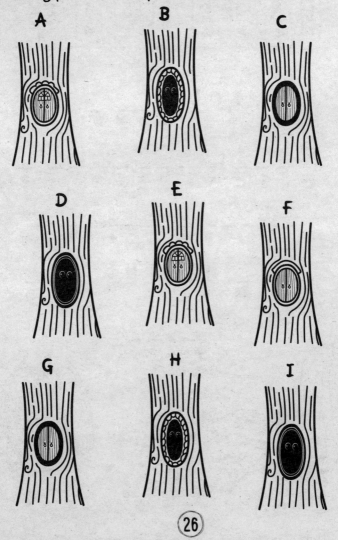

A

B

C

D

E

F

G

H

I

You've found the three remaining lockets, but nothing is happening. The Eerie Deerie is still here, stuck in the forest. Shouldn't they be disappearing or something?

In the word-wheels, find three emotion words. Each word starts with the centre letter and uses all the letters in the wheel once.

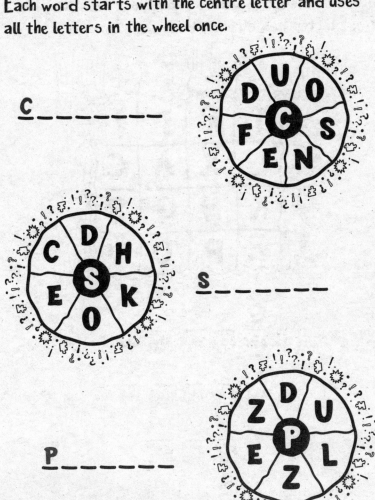

C _ _ _ _ _ _ _ _

S _ _ _ _ _ _

P _ _ _ _ _ _

Hmm... the Eerie Deerie did once hear a rumour about a long-lost relative they had forgotten about. Perhaps there is one more locket to find after all?

Use the grid references to work out each letter, then write them onto the lines below to reveal the name of the Eerie Deerie's long-lost relative. The first letter has already been done for you.

If there is another locket, it must be hidden somewhere else – you have already searched the Forever Forest from top to bottom!

Solve the number problem below each letter in the Key, then use the answers to fill in the gaps and reveal a message. Some letters have been done for you.

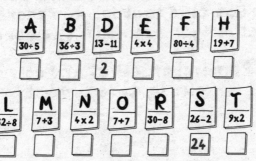

A	B	D	E	F	H
30÷5	36÷3	13–11	4×4	80÷4	19+7
		2			

L	M	N	O	R	S	T
32÷8	7+3	4×2	7+7	30–8	26–2	9×2
					24	

PL __ __ SE   S __ __ __ C __   THE
   16 6   24   24 16 6 22   26

__ __ ST OF THE   __ __ __ __ __
22 16 24   10 6 8 14 22

G __ __ U __ D S FOR THE
 22 14   8 2 24

LAST LOCKET.   __ __ Y __ __ IF
             10 6   12 16

YOU __ I __ D IT, THEN I'LL
    20   8 2

__ I __ __ __ __ Y BE   __ __ __ __ ...
20 8 6 4 4   20 22 16 16

29

Clue Logbook: Ghost One

Before you continue on your ghost-hunting adventure, take a minute to use this logbook to record any clues you found in the forest.

Remember, clues are pointed out by this symbol:

Note the clue letter next to the page number you found it on:

Page: 13   Clue letter: ◯

Page: 19   Clue letter: ◯

Page: 20   Clue letter: ◯

Page: 21   Clue letter: ◯

Page: 25   Clue letter: ◯

Page: 28   Clue letter: ◯

* Notes *

(Blank 'notes' pages like this are handy
for jotting down any notes or working
out when you're busy solving puzzles!

You could also use them
to write, doodle or
anything else you'd
like to do while on
your quest!)

GHOST TWO

Well done on finding the first ghost!

There is still a whole lot more ghost hunting to be done...

Who knows where this journey will take you next!?

Get ready for all kinds of word and number fun including tower tasks, palette puzzles and garden games!

Now it's time to seek spirit number two.
They say hunting ghosts is an art.
Whether that's true, is up to you,
But it's time to do your part...

?

Now let's find out the location of the second ghost to hunt...

Complete the number problems on each tower and write your answers into the circles. Each tower should have the same answer. The odd one out is the location of the next ghost. Which is it?

A

41 - 7

= ◯

The Shower Tower

B

17 x 2

= ◯

The Clock Tower

C

18 + 16

= ◯

The Boring Tower

D

11 x 4

= ◯

The Painting Tower

The Tower you need to get to is within the Secret
Garden... which is within the Walled Garden!

Can you make your way through the maze to the
Secret Garden in the centre?

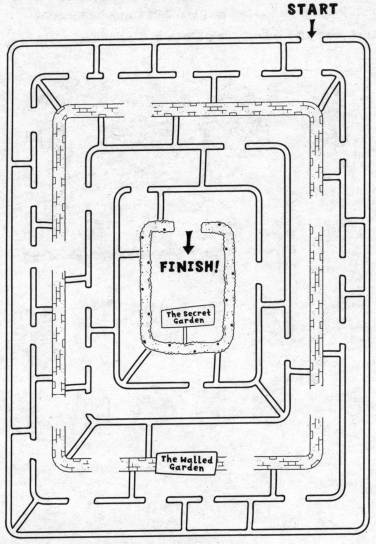

START

FINISH!

The Secret
Garden

The Walled
Garden

The Secret Garden is bursting with exotic and mysterious plants and flowers. As you explore it, your meter starts to detect a paranormal energy!

Make your way from start to finish. You can move up, down or sideways but you can't move diagonally and you must follow the plants in this order:

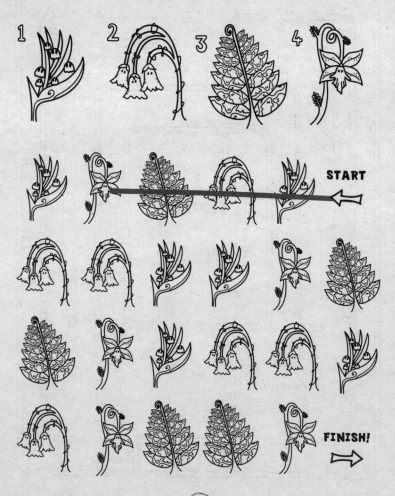

START

FINISH!

With your spectre binoculars you can see that you are getting closer to the paranormal force, which is radiating from the top of the tower...

Which of the tangled garden paths will lead you all the way to the tower?

As you get closer, you realise that the tower is surrounded by a moat and three bridges.

Follow the numbers along each bridge from left to right and figure out which number is next in the sequence. Write the final numbers into the boxes.

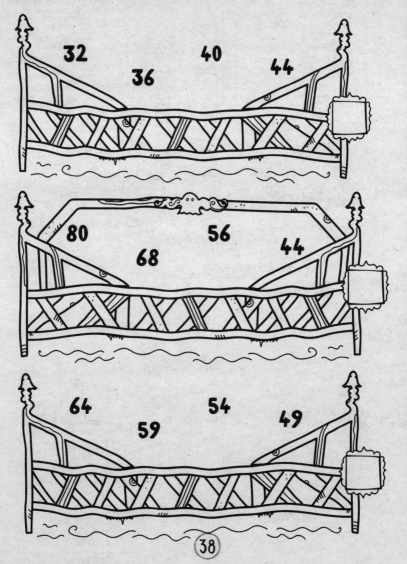

32   36   40   44

80   68   56   44

64   59   54   49

Inside the tower, the first thing you notice is that the walls are completely covered with frames of all shapes and sizes.

The numbers 1, 2, 3 and 4 should be added to each row, each column and each 2x2 bold outlined box, but should only appear once in each one.

This tower obviously used to be the art studio of a great painter – it is full of art supplies! It looks like they haven't been used for a long time now though...

In the word-wheels, find three things an artist might use. Each word starts with the centre letter and uses all the letters in the wheel once.

C _ _ _ _ _ _ _

B _ _ _ _ _ _ _
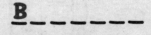

P _ _ _ _ _ _ _
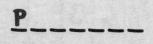

You climb the tower staircase looking at all of the paintings as you walk by. There are paintings of all sorts of things, including some that you recognise as being parts of the Wight Manor grounds and gardens.

Odd one out: which painting does not have a matching pair? Circle your answer.

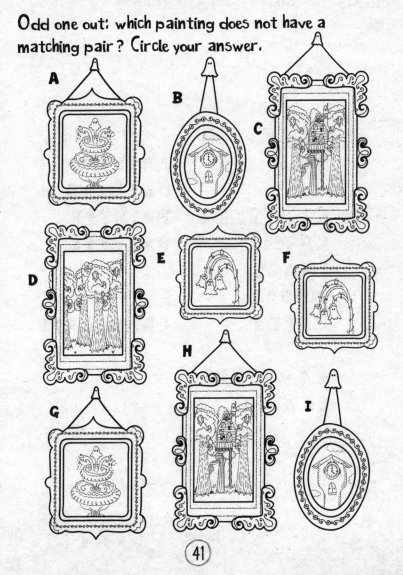

A

B

C

D

E

F

G

H

I

This sure does seem like a strange place for a spirit to haunt, but your ghost-hunting tools never lie — there is definitely a ghost somewhere in this painting tower!

Perhaps the ghost is an artist...?

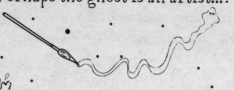

4 LETTERS
OILS

5 LETTERS
EASEL
IMAGE
MURAL
PAPER

6 LETTERS
SKETCH

7 LETTERS
ARTWORK
DRAWING
PAINTER
PALETTE

9 LETTERS
LANDSCAPE

Place each of the artist words from the list on the opposite page into the empty squares to create a filled crossword grid. Each word is used once so cross it off the list as you place it to help you keep track.

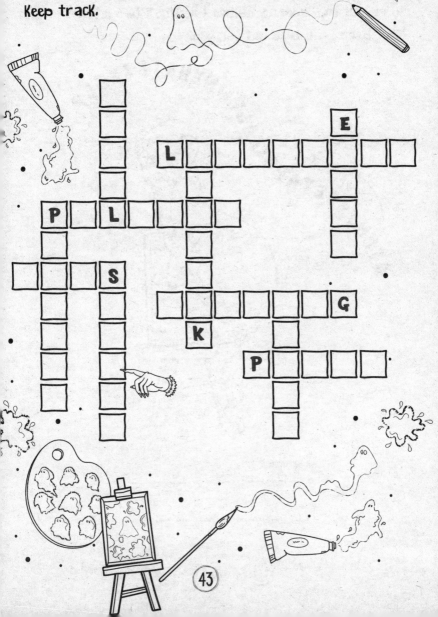

43

At the top of the tower, you find the second ghost!

Scribble out every other letter from left to right.
Write the letters that are left over onto the lines below
to reveal this ghost's name. The first two letters
have been scribbled out for you.

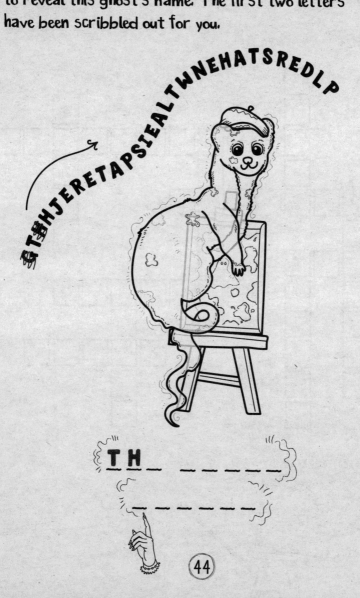

GTBHJERETAPSIEALTWNEHATSREDLP

T H _ _ _ _ _ _ _

_ _ _ _ _ _ _

What sort of unfinished business could this ghostly paint-covered weasel possibly have that would be keeping them stuck inside this tower...?

Follow the tangled lines and write the letter from the circle into the space at the other end of the line to fill in the gaps and discover the ghost's 'unfinished business'...

IF YOU'RE (H)(E)(R)(E) (T)(O) HELP ME,

I'M IN (L)(U)(C)(K).

IN (T)(H)(I)(S) ◯◯ W◯◯,

I AM ◯◯◯◯◯!

IN LIFE I (L)(O)(V)(E)(D) ART (T)(H)(E) (M)(O)(S)(T),

BUT BRUSHES CAN'T BE ◯◯◯◯◯ BY A

G◯◯◯◯.

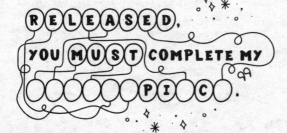

IF I AM TO BE

(R)(E)(L)(E)(A)(S)(E)(D),

(Y)(O)(U) (M)(U)(S)(T) COMPLETE MY

◯◯◯◯◯◯ P I C ◯.

To complete the weasel's final painting, you will need to collect flowers from the Secret Garden that you can use to make paint colours.

Travel the paths to visit each flower garden once. Only use one straight line to connect each flower and whatever you do, don't travel along the same path twice!

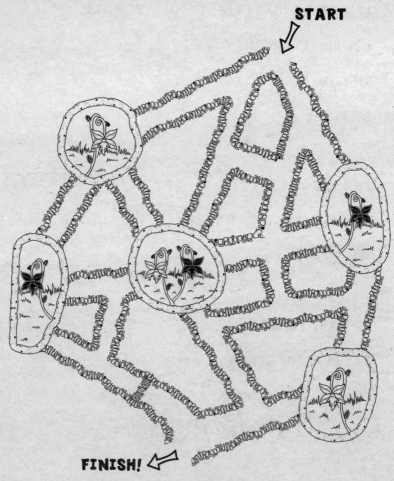

START

FINISH!

Now it's time to make the two special paint colours you'll need to complete the masterpiece: 'Ghostly White' and 'Phantom Black'.

To turn the flowers into pigment powder and mix the pigments into paint, make your way from start to finish. You can move up, down or sideways, but you can't move diagonally and you must only follow even numbers.

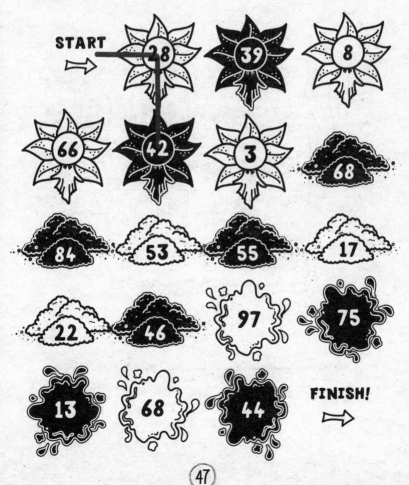

While you're out collecting flowers in the garden, you also uncover something else hidden in the soil!

A word has been hidden in the letter grid. Simply cross out any letter that appears more than once and write the letters that are left over onto the lines below in the order they appear. Letter W has been scribbled out to start you off.

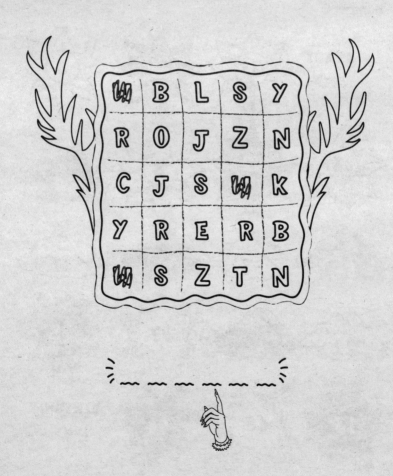

Use the symbol Key to crack the code and fill in the missing letters to find out what happens next... Some letters have already been done for you.

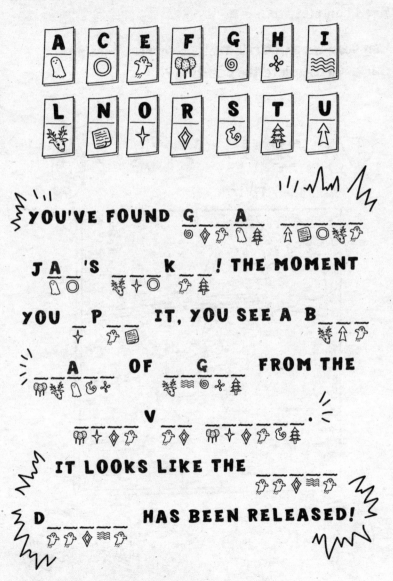

Symbol Key:
A | C | E | F | G | H | I
L | N | O | R | S | T | U

YOU'VE FOUND G _ _ A _ _   _ _ _ _ _

J A _ 'S   _ _ _ k _ _ !   THE MOMENT

YOU _ P _ _   IT, YOU SEE A   B _ _ _ _

_ _ _ A _   OF   _ _ G _ _   FROM THE

V _ _ _ _ _   _ _ _ _ _ _ _ _ .

IT LOOKS LIKE THE   _ _ _ _ _ _

D _ _ _ _ _ _   HAS BEEN RELEASED!

Back inside the Painting Tower, the Easel Weasel knows exactly what they want their masterpiece to look like. There are a few unfinished parts that still need completing...

Can you find and circle the two correct missing parts to complete the painting?

Nearly there! Before you present it to the weasel, you go through their checklist to make sure the painting contains everything they asked for.

Can you find and circle all the things from the list below in the painting above?

 4 Paint Palettes

 5 Square Frames

 6 Art Easels

 7 Painting Hats

 7 Oval Frames

 8 Paint Brushes

You have completed the Easel Weasel's masterpiece!
Now all that's left to do is to give it a title...

Follow the lines and write the letter from the
oval into the space at the other end of the line
to reveal a new word. Some of the letters have
already been done for you.

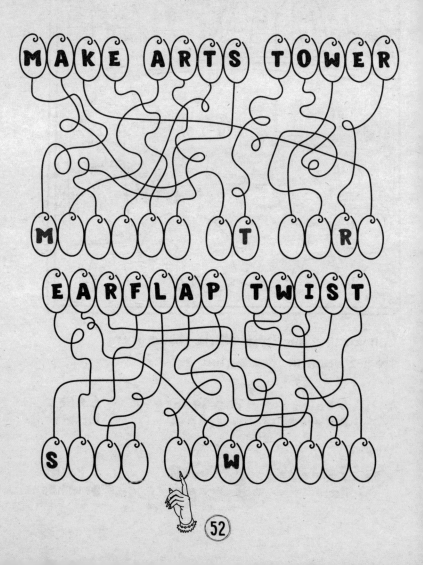

What will happen to the weasel now that their unfinished business is complete?

Solve the number problem below each letter in the Key, then use the answers to fill in the gaps and reveal the weasel's message. One letter has been done for you.

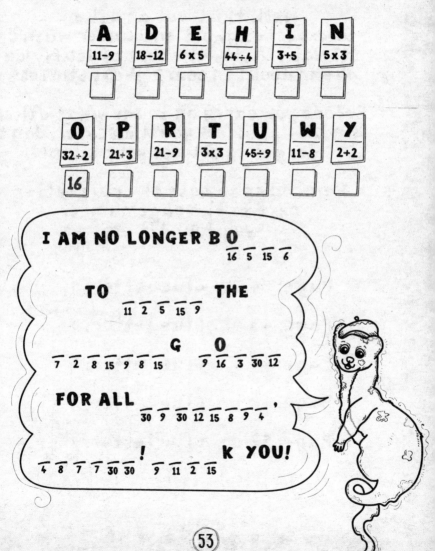

A 11-9	**D** 18-12	**E** 6 x 5	**H** 44÷4	**I** 3+5	**N** 5 x 3

O 32÷2	**P** 21÷3	**R** 21-9	**T** 3 x 3	**U** 45÷9	**W** 11-8	**Y** 2+2
16						

I AM NO LONGER B O _ _ _ _
16 5 15 6

TO _ _ _ _ _ THE
11 2 5 15 9

_ _ _ _ _ _ G _ O _ _
7 2 8 15 9 8 15   9 16 3 30 12

FOR ALL _ _ _ _ _ _ _ _ ,
30 9 30 12 15 8 9 4

_ _ _ _ _ _ ! _ _ _ K YOU!
4 8 7 7 30 30   9 11 2 15

Clue Logbook:
Ghost Two

Well, that was a rather
unexpected ghost encounter wasn't
it? Not exactly the sort of stuff you
hear about in scary ghost stories!

Before you carry on to see what other
kinds of ghosties you'll discover, don't
forget to collect your clues!

Remember to note the clue letter
next to the page number
you found it on:

Page: 34   Clue letter: ◯

Page: 43   Clue letter: ◯

Page: 44   Clue letter: ◯

Page: 48   Clue letter: ◯

Page: 52   Clue letter: ◯

* Notes *

GHOST THREE

How are you enjoying your ghost-hunting quest?

You seem to be getting good at it!

In the next part of your adventure, be ready to crack some cable car conundrums and have some fountain fun.

You will also be taking on watery word games and torchlit tasks!

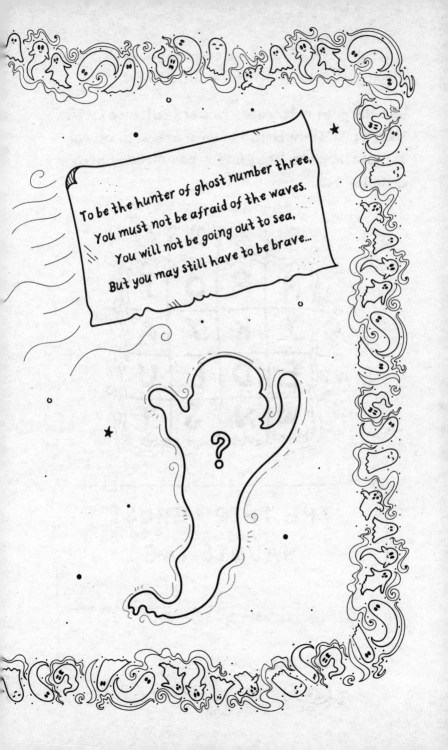

To be the hunter of ghost number three,
You must not be afraid of the waves.
You will not be going out to sea,
But you may still have to be brave...

Two ghosts found, three more to go! It's time to discover the location of the third ghost...

Use the grid references to work out each letter, then write them onto the lines below to reveal the location. The first letter has already been done for you.

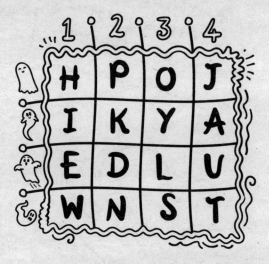

THE THIRD GHOST HAUNTS THE

S __ __ __ __ __ __   __ __ __ __

Walking all the way there will take ages!
Why not hop onto the rusty Old Cable Car instead?

Follow the numbers along each cable car wire from
left to right and figure out which number is next in
the sequence. Write the final numbers into the boxes.

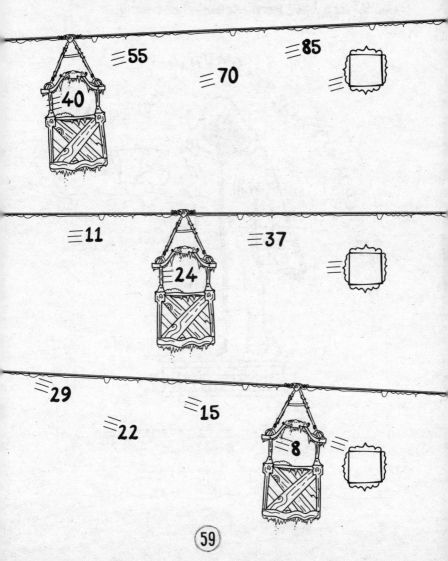

40   55   70   85   □

11   24   37   □

29   22   15   8   □

Your cable car ride comes to an end in the Statue Gardens, so you ask one of the statues for directions.

Scribble out every other letter from left to right. Write the letters that are left over onto the lines below to reveal the statue's instructions. The first two letters have been scribbled out for you.

F O _ _ _ _   _ _ _

_ _ _ _ _ _ _ _ _

Make your way from start to finish. You can move up, down or sideways but you can't move diagonally and you must follow the fountains in this order:

1 **2** **3** **4**

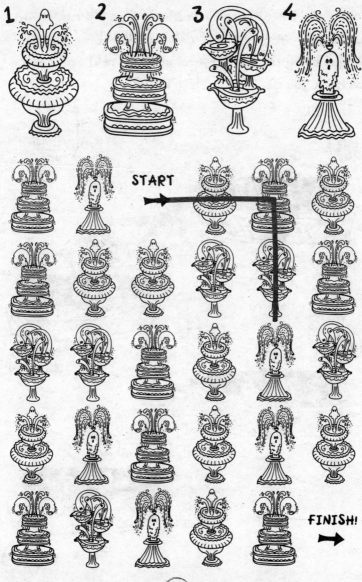

START

FINISH!

The fountains lead you all the way to the shore of a dark and misty lake, with four rowing boats moored next to it.

Complete the number problems in each boat and write your answers into the circles. Each boat should have the same answer. The odd one out is the boat you get into... which is it?

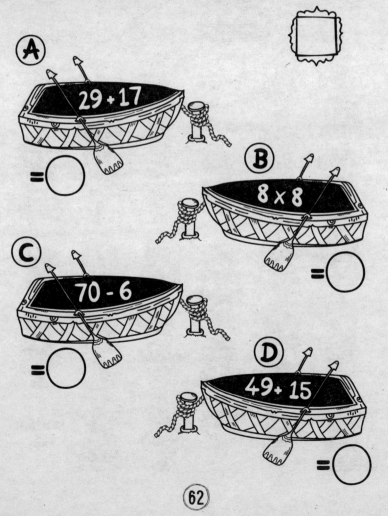

Ⓐ

29 + 17

=◯

Ⓑ

8 × 8

=◯

Ⓒ

70 - 6

=◯

Ⓓ

49 + 15

=◯

Can you row your boat through the maze to the centre of the lake?

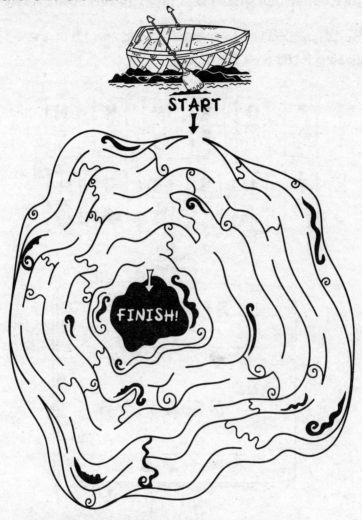

As you row, a dark night falls around you. The further you go, the blacker the water and shadowy mist become, until you can barely see anything...

Just as you begin to pass multiple warning signs, your whisperphone starts picking up creepy noises.

Use the symbol Key to crack the code and fill in the missing letters on the sign...

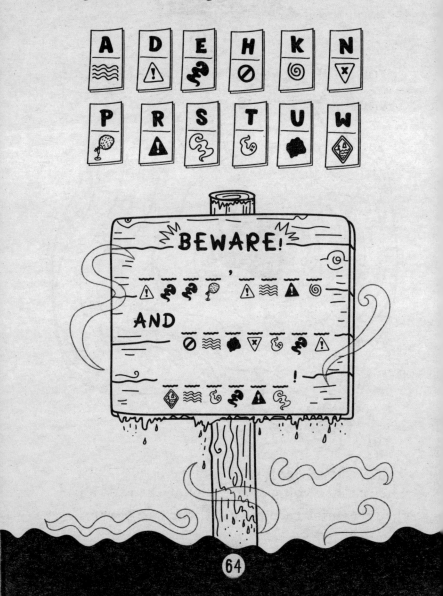

Suddenly, a ghost rises from the water! Their voice echoes around you as they sing a scary song...

Follow the tangled lines and write the letter from the circle into the space at the other end of the line to fill in the gaps and discover the ghostly warning song...

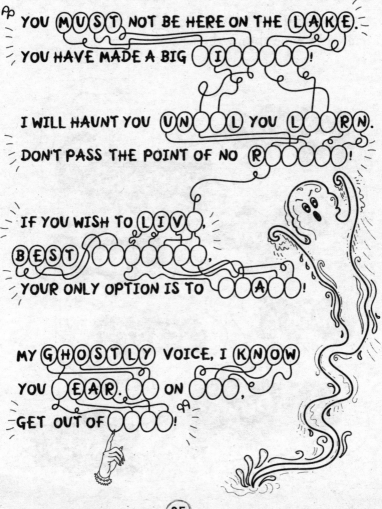

YOU (M)(U)(S)(T) NOT BE HERE ON THE (L)(A)(K)(E).

YOU HAVE MADE A BIG ()(I)()()()()!

I WILL HAUNT YOU (U)(N)()()(L) YOU (L)()()(R)(N).

DON'T PASS THE POINT OF NO (R)()()()()!

IF YOU WISH TO (L)(I)(V)(),

(B)(E)(S)(T)()()()()(),

YOUR ONLY OPTION IS TO ()()(A)()!

MY (G)(H)(O)(S)(T)(L)(Y) VOICE, I (K)(N)(O)(W)

YOU ()(E)(A)(R). ()() ON ()()(),

GET OUT OF ()()()()!

You row away as fast as you can! As you move through the gloomy shadows, you feel scared and all alone on this dark lake.

But, you'll never be able to complete the ghost's unfinished business if you don't talk to them...

No matter how much they warned you, your only option might just be to find the courage to turn back and face them... be brave!

Can you find all eight of the lake words from the list on the opposite page in the wordsearch below?

Words may be hidden horizontally or vertically.

```
T S H A D O W S E N M
B C D Q P T F S P H S
C O M R U H B Z Q E C
R Q U N I G L O O M A
E W R V M R R K W Z R
E E K S E S C I A R Y
P K Y A S E R N V J C
Y S P O S Q Y G E S I
E D A R K N E S S O E
R C O B Y O N L O R N
W M I S T Y G Z Q R T
```

When you go back for the second time, the ghost looks a lot less scary. Actually, it looks a little sad...

Follow the lines and write the letter from each oval into the space at the other end of the line to reveal the ghost's name. The first letter of each word has already been done for you...

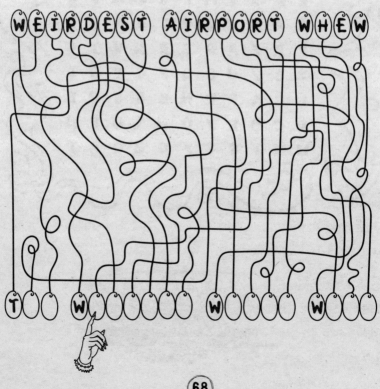

WEIRDEST AIRPORT WHEW

T _ _   W _ _ _ _ _   W _ _ _   W _ _

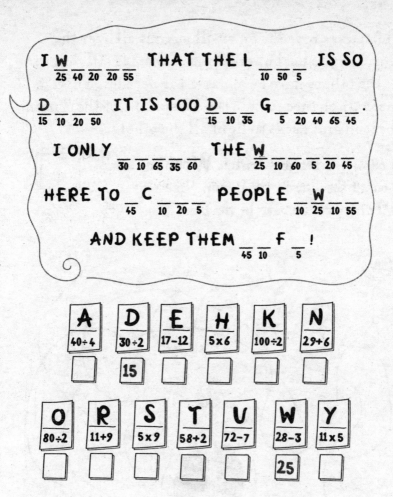

Now that things seem to have calmed down a bit, you can finally ask the third ghost about their unfinished business...

Solve the number problem below each letter in the key, then use the answers to fill in the gaps and reveal the message above. Some letters have been done for you.

There are beacons on small islands all over the Shadowy Lake, but only one of them is still burning – the others have been dark for decades. This could be your chance to help the Wisp! Collect the flaming beacon and use it to light all the others...

Follow the tangled routes. Which one leads you all the way to the flaming beacon? Write your answer in the box.

You follow the Wisp to island after island, using your flaming torch to light beacons and bonfires.

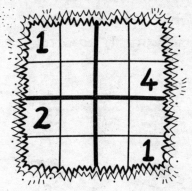

The numbers 1, 2, 3 and 4 should be added to each row, each column and each 2x2 bold outlined box, but should only appear once in each one.

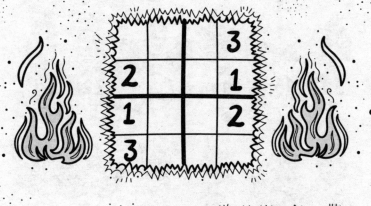

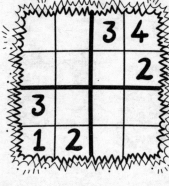

Continue your mission to set each beacon ablaze!

Make your way through the beacons from start to finish. You can move up, down or sideways, but you can't move diagonally and you must only follow the odd numbers.

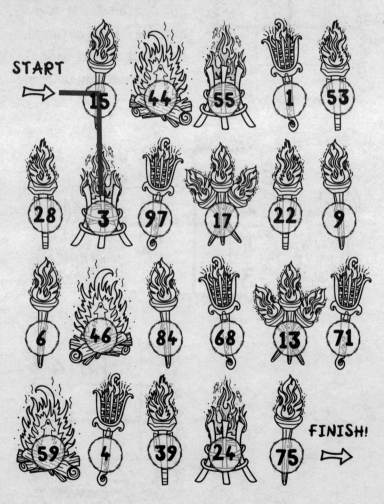

You've nearly done it, there aren't many left to light now...

Travel the routes to visit each beacon once. Only use one straight line to connect each beacon and whatever you do, don't travel along the same route twice!

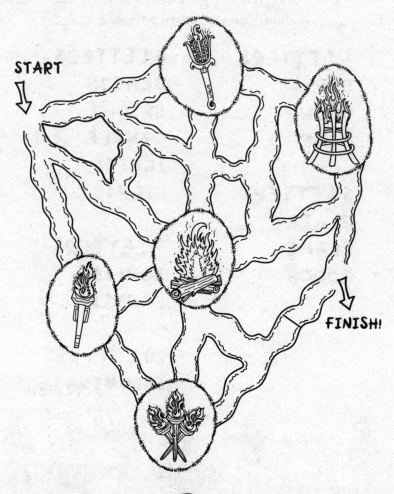

START

FINISH!

As the fire of each beacon burns brighter, slowly but surely the gloomy darkness that once hung over the Shadowy Lake starts to lift.

Soon, it's light enough to see that the lake is full of gigantic koi fish! They were swimming around under your boat this whole time and you had no idea! Their bright orange scales glow so brilliantly, they almost look like swimming flames.

4 LETTERS
BURN
GLOW
LAMP

5 LETTERS
BLAZE
FLAME
TORCH

6 LETTERS
BEACON
BRIGHT
CANDLE
IGNITE
LIGHTS

7 LETTERS
BONFIRE
LANTERN

10 LETTERS
ILLUMINATE

Place each of the fiery words from the list on the opposite page into the empty squares to create a filled crossword grid. Each word is used once so cross it off the list as you place it to help you keep track.

You did it! You lit up the Shadowy Lake and made it a much safer place. Thanks to you, the Worried Water Wisp no longer has to worry!

In the word-wheels, find three emotion words that are the opposite of 'worried'. Each word starts with the centre letter and uses all the letters in the wheel once.

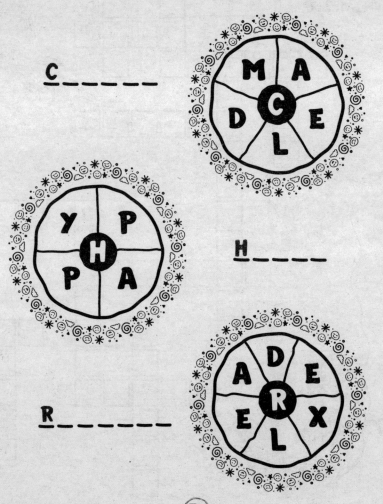

C _ _ _ _ _ _

H _ _ _ _

R _ _ _ _ _ _ _

Use the grid references to work out each letter, then fill in the gaps below to reveal a message from the Wisp. Some letters have already been done for you.

	1	2	3	4
	L	N	C	W
	Y	A	H	U
	G	S	K	J
	E	O	X	M

I CAN FINALLY REST.
THANK YOU FOR YOUR HELP!
HEY, I GUESS THIS MEANS
WE'LL HAVE TO C _ _ _ _ _
      3🐉 3🐉 2🔥 2🐉 1🐉

_ Y _ _ _ _ _ _ AND THE
4🐉 1🔥 2🐉 2🐉 4🐉 1🐉

_ _ _ _ _ OF THE _ _ _ _ ! I'LL
2🐉 2🐉 4🐉 1🐉   1🐉 2🐉 3〰 1🐉

LEAVE Y _ _ TO C _ _ _ _ _
      1🔥 2🐉 4🔥   3🐉 3🐉 2🐉 2🐉 2〰 1🐉

THE _ _ _ _ _ _ _ _ _ ...
    2🐉 1🐉 4🐉 2🐉 2🐉 2🐉 4🐉 1🐉 2〰

Clue Logbook:
Ghost Three

Phew! That ghost was a bit scarier than the last one, but luckily not scary for long.

You've still got a whole haunted manor to explore and at least two more ghosts to find...

Before you carry on, remember to record your clues so far!

Note the clue letter next to the page number you found it on:

Page: 60   Clue letter: ◯

Page: 65   Clue letter: ◯

Page: 68   Clue letter: ◯

Page: 70   Clue letter: ◯

Page: 77   Clue letter: ◯

* Notes *

GHOST FOUR

Are you ready to explore the next mysterious location in search of another curious ghost?

You'd better be!

In this part of your journey, you'll be facing manor mind games and password puzzles...

You will also find room riddles and messy mysteries, web word games and noble number fun!

In pursuit of spirit number four,
A mystery must you settle.
A great mess you will explore,
For the ghost made of metal...

Three ghosts found and released! You're pretty good at this ghost-hunting thing! Hmm, where could the next ghost be lurking...?

Solve the number problem below each letter in the Key, then use the answers to fill in the gaps and reveal the location. Two letters have been done for you.

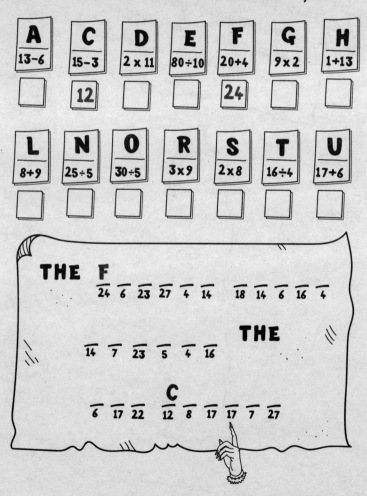

A	C	D	E	F	G	H
13–6	15–3	2 x 11	80÷10	20+4	9 x 2	1+13
	12			24		

L	N	O	R	S	T	U
8+9	25÷5	30÷5	3 x 9	2 x 8	16÷4	17+6

THE F $\overline{24}$ $\overline{6}$ $\overline{23}$ $\overline{27}$ $\overline{4}$ $\overline{14}$ $\overline{18}$ $\overline{14}$ $\overline{6}$ $\overline{16}$ $\overline{4}$

$\overline{14}$ $\overline{7}$ $\overline{23}$ $\overline{5}$ $\overline{4}$ $\overline{16}$ THE

$\overline{6}$ $\overline{17}$ $\overline{22}$ C $\overline{12}$ $\overline{8}$ $\overline{17}$ $\overline{17}$ $\overline{7}$ $\overline{27}$

Use the wooden walkway (also known as the 'Bendy Boardwalk') to get all the way across Banshee Bog.

Follow the numbers along the walkway and figure out the number sequence. Fill in the blank circles with the correct numbers to complete the number sequence.

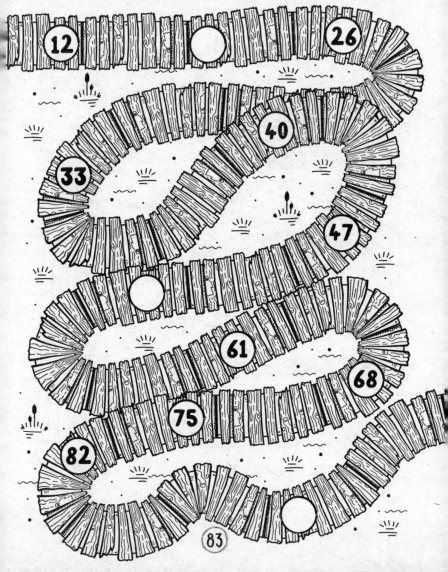

The best way to get to the manor house is to go
through the Hedge Maze... try not to get lost!

Can you make your way through the maze to reach
Wight Manor on the other side?

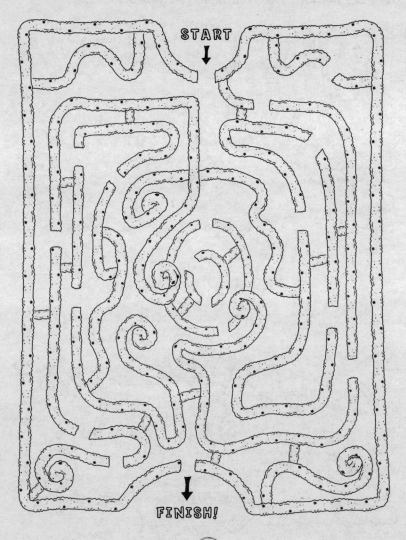

START

FINISH!

Can you spot all eight differences between these two pictures of Wight Manor?

To enter into the Great Entrance Hall of Wight Manor, you must say both passwords out loud.

Follow the lines and write the letter from each oval into the space at the other end of the line to reveal both passwords. The first letter of each word has already been done for you.

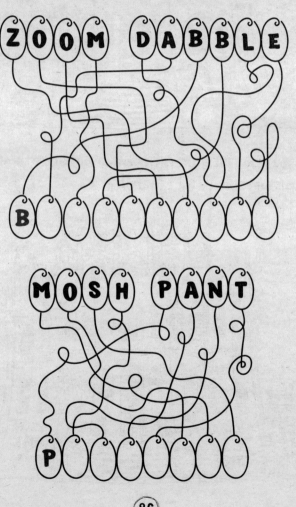

The Great Entrance Hall is a large, round room with so many different doors to choose from!

Find out which door leads to which room by solving the number problems in the box below each door. Then draw a line to match each door to the correct answer. One has already been done for you.

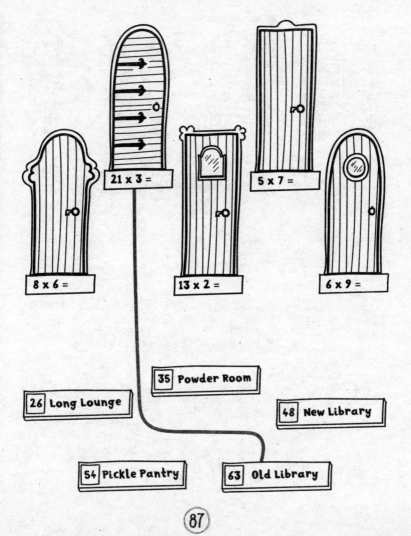

21 x 3 =

5 x 7 =

8 x 6 =

13 x 2 =

6 x 9 =

35 Powder Room

26 Long Lounge

48 New Library

54 Pickle Pantry

63 Old Library

Your phantom frequency radio is picking up on a ghostly signal! You follow it all the way through the door and to the back of the Long Lounge.

Make your way from start to finish. You can move up, down or sideways but you can't move diagonally and you must follow the lounge items in this order:

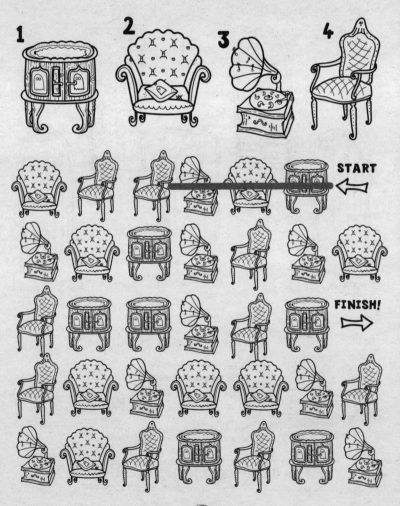

1 **2** **3** **4**

START ⟵

FINISH! ⟹

At the end of the Long Lounge, you find four openings in the floor with ladders leading deep down into darkness...

Complete the number problem in each opening and write your answers into the circles.
Each ladder should have the same answer.
The odd one out is the one you climb down. Which is it?

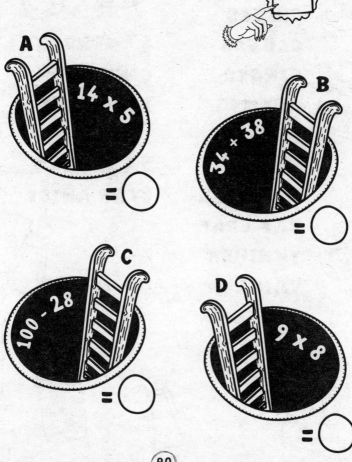

A   14 x 5   = ◯

B   34 + 38   = ◯

C   100 - 28   = ◯

D   9 x 8   = ◯

At the bottom of the ladder you find yourself in a tall room with floor-to-ceiling shelves full of jars!

The jars contain all kinds of leaves, seeds and colourful powders. You must be in the Herbs and Spices Pantry...

6 LETTERS

CHIVES
CLOVES
GINGER
NUTMEG
PEPPER

8 LETTERS

CINNAMON
ROSEMARY

9 LETTERS

STAR ANISE

7 LETTERS

BAY LEAF
JUNIPER
VANILLA
OREGANO

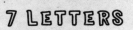

Place each of the herbs and spices words from the list on the opposite page into the empty squares to create a filled crossword grid. Each word is used once so cross it off the list as you place it to help you keep track.

The phantom radio signal is getting stronger. It leads you through messy rooms full of old items and storage boxes. Could this be the Old Cellar?

Make your way from start to finish. You can move up, down or sideways but you can't move diagonally and you must follow the items in this order:

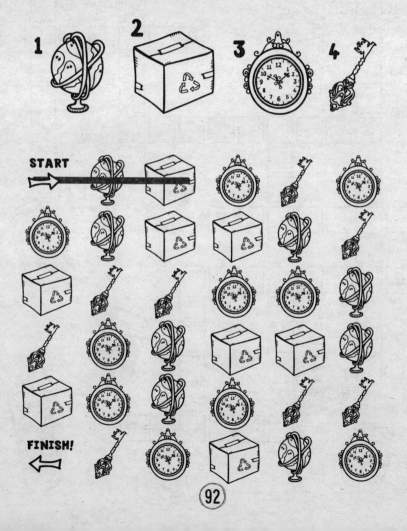

This seems a place for long-forgotten things that have been down here for many years. All was silent a moment ago, but now you hear a strange noise... is that the sound of someone crying?

Can you find all eight of the words from the list in the wordsearch below? Words may be hidden horizontally or vertically.

- ANCIENT
- COBWEBS
- CRYING
- DUSTY
- FORGOTTEN
- MESSY
- SOBBING
- WEEPING

```
T F O R G O T T E N M
B C D U P T F S P H S
W O U R U H B O Q E M
H B S N I Z H B R F X
P W T V M R R B O Z A
E E Y S E S C I Z R N
L B S A S E R N S J C
K S P O S S Y G E S I
E J E S Y H I R R O E
R C O B Y O N L O R N
W E E P I N G Z A R T
```

The weeping sounds are coming from that dusty old suit of armour... You've found the fourth ghost!

Scribble out every other letter from left to right. Write the letters that are left over onto the lines below to reveal this ghost's name. The first two letters have been scribbled out for you.

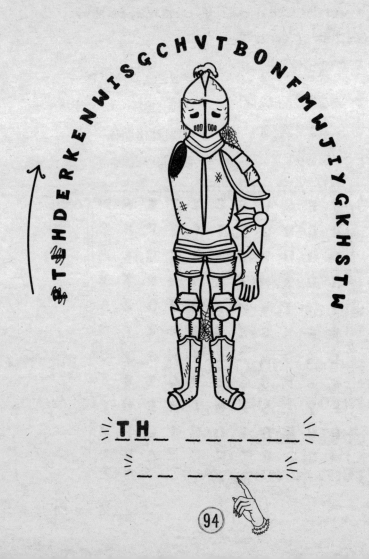

T H _ _ _ _ _ _ _

_ _ _ _ _ _ _

A ghost stuck inside a suit of armour? How unusual! What could it possibly want from you?

Follow the tangled lines and write the letter from the circle into the space at the other end of the line to fill in the gaps and discover the ghost's 'unfinished business'...

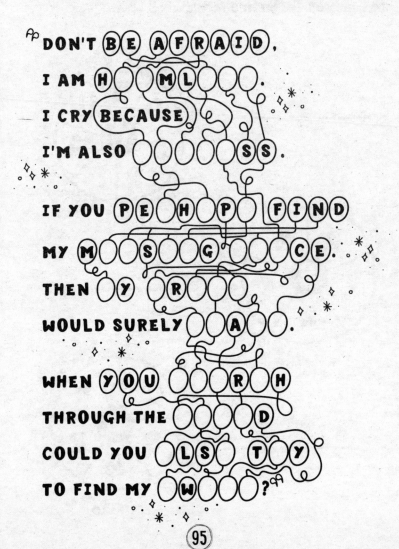

DON'T BE AFRAID,

I AM H◯◯ML◯◯◯.

I CRY BECAUSE

I'M ALSO ◯◯◯◯◯◯SS.

IF YOU PE◯H◯P◯ FIND

MY M◯◯S◯◯G◯◯◯CE.

THEN ◯◯Y◯◯R◯◯◯◯

WOULD SURELY ◯◯A◯◯.

WHEN YOU ◯◯◯◯R◯H

THROUGH THE ◯◯◯◯◯D

COULD YOU ◯LS◯◯T◯Y

TO FIND MY ◯W◯◯◯?

You hunt through the Old Cellar for places where armour might be hidden.

In the word-wheels, find three things that might have something stored or hidden inside them. Each word starts with the centre letter and uses all the letters in the wheel once.

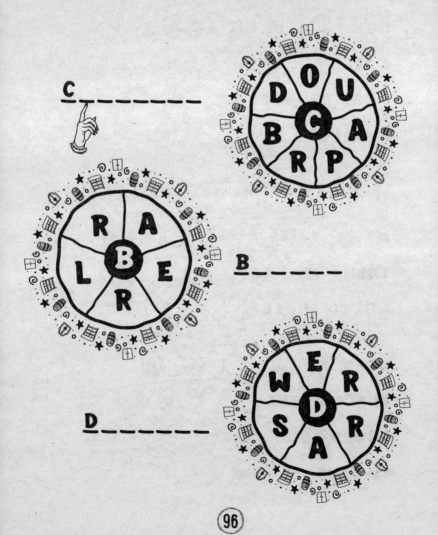

C _ _ _ _ _ _ _

B _ _ _ _ _ _

D _ _ _ _ _ _ _

You find nearly a whole army of armour stashed away down here! But which pieces do you really need?

Can you find and circle the three correct armour pieces to complete the Knight's full arm?
Here's what it should look like.

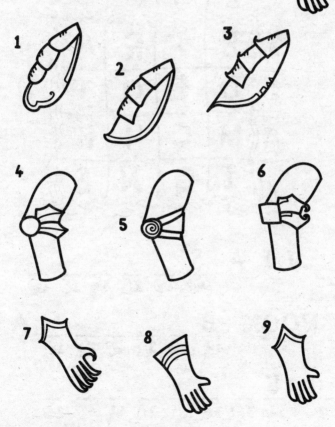

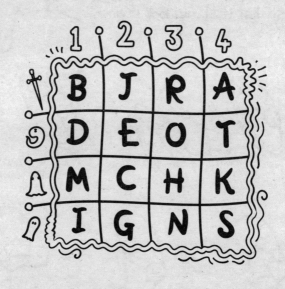

Next, you hunt for the Knight's sword...
Where you find it is rather unexpected!

Use the grid references to work out each letter,
then fill in the gaps below to reveal where you
find the sword. Some letters have already
been done for you.

1 2 3 4

	1	2	3	4
⚔	B	J	R	A
♪	D	E	O	T
🔔	M	C	H	K
👻	I	G	N	S

IN A S __ __ __ __ __
    4👻 2♪ 2🔔 3⚔ 2♪ 4♪

ROOM B __ __ __ __ __ A
    1⚔ 2♪ 3🔔 1👻 3👻 1♪

B __ __ __ __ __ __ S
1⚔ 3♪ 3♪ 4🔔 2🔔 4⚔ 4👻 2♪

In fact, you don't just find one sword in there, you discover an entire collection of swords!

Odd one out: the sword that doesn't have a matching pair is the sword that belongs to the Knight. Can you find and circle it?

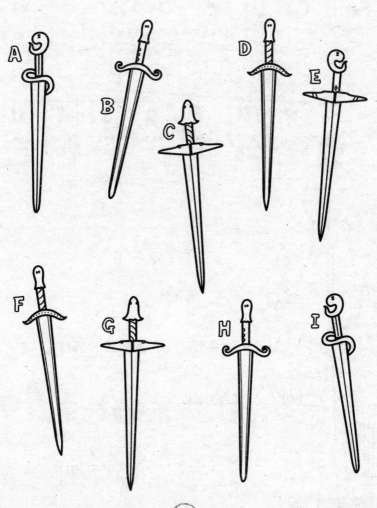

After putting their armour back together again, you give the Knight a nice clean and polish.

Solve the number problem below each letter in the Key, then use the answers to fill in the gaps and reveal the Knight's message. One letter has been done for you.

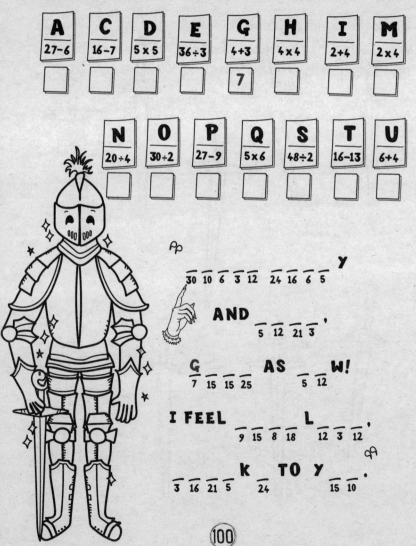

A	C	D	E	G	H	I	M
27–6	16–7	5 x 5	36÷12	4+3	4x4	2+4	2x4
				7			

N	O	P	Q	S	T	U
20÷4	30÷2	27–9	5x6	48÷2	16–13	6+4

$\overline{30}\ \overline{10}\ \overline{6}\ \overline{3}\ \overline{12}\ \overline{24}\ \overline{16}\ \overline{6}\ \overline{5}$ Y

AND $\overline{5}\ \overline{12}\ \overline{21}\ \overline{3}$,

G $\overline{7}\ \overline{15}\ \overline{15}\ \overline{25}$ AS $\overline{5}\ \overline{12}$ W!

I FEEL $\overline{9}\ \overline{15}\ \overline{8}\ \overline{18}$ L $\overline{12}\ \overline{3}\ \overline{12}$,

$\overline{3}\ \overline{16}\ \overline{21}\ \overline{5}$ K $\overline{24}$ TO Y $\overline{15}\ \overline{10}$.

100

The Knight tells you about a different way to get back up into the main part of Wight Manor:

"Hidden in the bookcase room, there are six levers. When you enter the correct number combination and pull them, a secret lift will appear!"

Solve the number problems and write the answers in the boxes at the end of the tangled lines. Then, the number combination for the lift will be revealed!

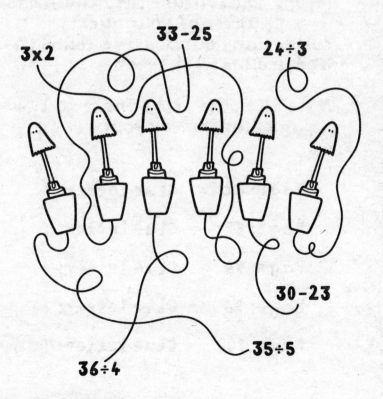

3x2

33-25

24÷3

30-23

35÷5

36÷4

Clue Logbook:
Ghost Four

Well, it seems like ghosts can be found haunting just about anything!
Who knew!?

Before you venture into the final chapter of your quest, collect any clues you've found in and around Wight Manor so far...

Note the clue letter next to the page number you found it on:

Page: 82   Clue letter: ◯

Page: 89   Clue letter: ◯

Page: 94   Clue letter: ◯

Page: 96   Clue letter: ◯

Page: 100   Clue letter: ◯

★ Notes ★

GHOST FIVE

What a journey
you've had so far!

You have definitely
levelled-up in the world
of ghost hunting...

You might just be
the best there is!

Test yourself one
more time with these
playful puzzles,
top-floor tasks,
round riddles
and lots more
floating fun!

In search of the ghost of five,
you may climb stair after stair.
Help spirits rise, bring them alive,
Come along, you're almost there...

Your quest is almost complete. Now it's time to discover where the final ghost is hiding...

Use the grid references to work out each letter, then fill in the gaps below to reveal the location. The first letters have already been done for you.

THE FINAL GHOSTS
HAUNT THE A ___ ___ ___ ___ ___
         1   2   2   3   4

P ___ ___ ___ ___ ___ ___ ___
3   1   1   3   4   2   2   3

The secret lift continues to take you up, up, up through the many floors of the Manor house...

The numbers 1, 2, 3 and 4 should be added to each row, each column and each 2x2 bold outlined box, but should only appear once in each one.

You travel up in the lift until you reach what seems to be the highest floor of the Manor.

This place sure does have a lot of different kinds of rooms! You search through each room type, keeping a close eye on your ghost-hunting gadgets, hoping to detect something...

Can you find all eight of the room types from the list on the opposite page in the wordsearch below?

Words may be hidden horizontally or vertically.

T	R	B	G	U	M	U	S	I	C	M
B	C	E	E	P	T	F	B	P	H	S
W	L	D	R	U	H	B	R	Q	E	R
Z	E	R	N	I	O	H	T	R	F	E
E	A	O	V	W	R	R	U	O	O	A
Q	N	O	S	E	S	E	P	Z	R	D
L	E	M	P	D	I	N	I	N	G	I
K	R	P	A	B	S	T	A	E	S	N
E	J	E	R	T	H	R	R	R	O	G
R	C	D	E	C	G	U	E	S	T	O
L	A	U	N	D	R	Y	S	A	R	X
T	S	I	T	T	I	N	G	A	R	X

Next, you explore the bathroom, which is less like a room and more like an entire bathhouse...

This place is ginormous, with all kinds of hot and cold baths, showers, fountains and even a big bubble machine!

SPA

JETS
POOL
SINK

TOWEL
WATER

HOT TAP
SHOWER
SPLASH

COLD TAP

FOUNTAIN

BUBBLEBATH

Place each of the bath words from the list on the opposite page into the empty squares to create a filled crossword grid. Each word is used once so cross it off the list as you place it to help you keep track.

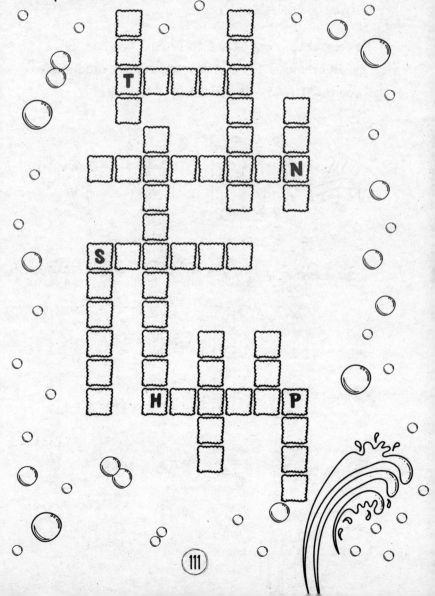

What's next? Another bedroom!? But wait, this room isn't like the others... your ectoplasm detector is beeping and your field meter is flashing!

Somewhere in this room, there must be a hidden entrance to the Attic Playroom...

Make your way from start to finish. You can move up, down or sideways but you can't move diagonally and you must follow the items in this order:

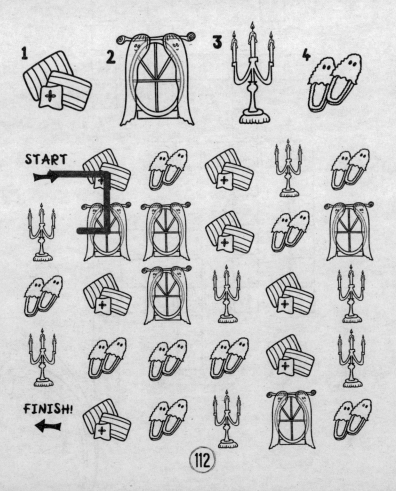

Can you spot all seven differences between these two pictures of the ghostly bedroom?

Use the grid references to work out each letter, then fill in the gaps below to reveal the location of the hidden entrance. The first letters have already been done for you.

THE ENTRANCE TO
THE ATTIC IS HIDDEN

B _ _ _ _ _ THE
4✳ 2◉ 3★ 1★ 4☖ 1✳

F _ _ _ _ _ _ _ _
4★ 1★ 2★ 2◉ 1☖ 1◉ 3✳ 3☖ 2◉

Inside the hidden entrance, you find rope ladders leading up to an even higher floor, how curious!

Follow the numbers up the rope ladders from bottom to top and figure out which number is next in the sequence. Write the final numbers into the boxes.

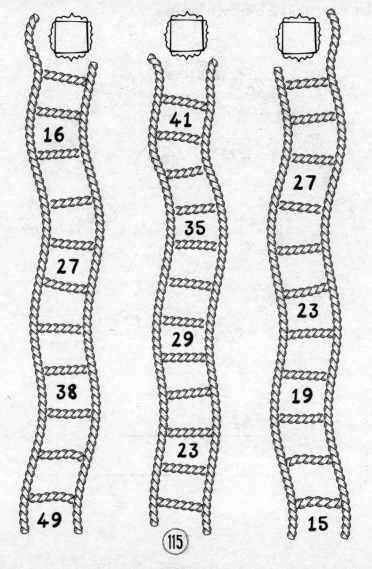

16

27

38

49

41

35

29

23

27

23

19

15

The rope ladders lead you up into an attic, lit up by glowing, floating, ghostly blobs!

Scribble out every other letter from left to right. Write the letters that are left over onto the lines below to reveal their message. The first two letters have been scribbled out for you.

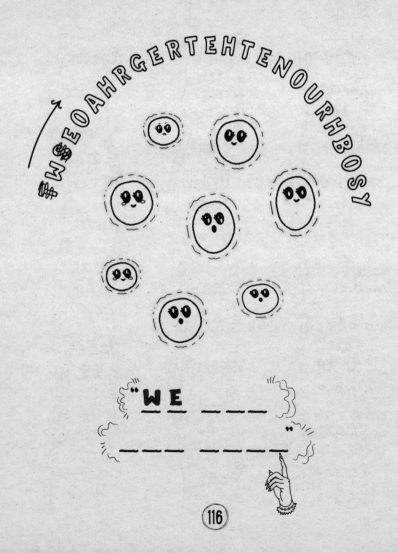

Just when you thought you were about to find the fifth and final ghost, you found a whole bunch of little ghosts!

Follow the tangled lines and write the letter from the circle into the space at the other end of the line to fill in the gaps and discover the orbs' 'unfinished business'...

"WE ARE GHOSTS WITH NO (S)(H)(E)(L)(L),

THINGS TO HAUNT WOULD BE (W)⃝⃝⃝.

SOME OF US WANT (H)⃝(T),

THAT WOULD REALLY BE ⃝⃝⃝⃝⃝.

FOR SOME, TO BECOME A ⃝(O)(Y)

WOULD (B)(R)(I)(N)(G) SO MUCH (J)⃝⃝.

TO HAVE A (D)⃝(S)⃝(U)⃝(S)(E)

WOULD BE THE (T)(R)⃝⃝ (P)(R)⃝(Z)⃝.

CAN YOU FIND US SOMEWHERE TO (H)⃝⃝⃝?

WE'D BE GRATEFUL IF YOU (T)(R)⃝⃝⃝!"

One of the orb ghosts would love to be a teddy bear, so you look through the toys in the attic to find the perfect teddy bear for them to haunt.

Which silhouette correctly matches each teddy bear? Circle your answers.

Lots of the orbs dream about being classic ghosties — you know the ones: spooky little things covered in draped sheets or blankets. But they don't want boring plain white sheets, they want to be fun, patterned ghosts!

Odd one out: which patterned sheet or blanket does not have a matching pair? Circle your answer.

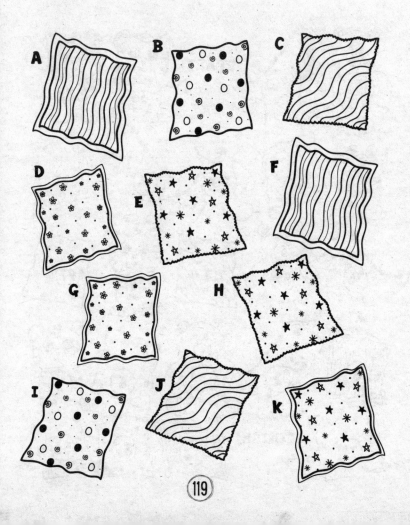

It takes a while to find the perfect item for each orb to inhabit. They all have such weird and wonderful requests for the types of toys and items they'd like to haunt.

You can move up, down or sideways, but you can't move diagonally and you must only follow the items with odd numbers...

One orb would absolutely love to haunt the perfect rocking horse!

Complete the number problems above each rocking horse and write your answers into the circles. Each horse should have the same answer. The odd one out is the horse the orb chooses. Which one is it?

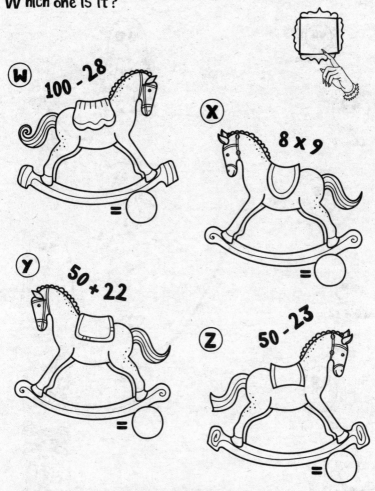

W 100 - 28
=

X 8 × 9
=

Y 50 + 22
=

Z 50 - 23
=

Now each orb has something to haunt, it's time for their spirits to get comfy in their new shells...

Match the orbs to their new shells by solving the number problem below each orb. Then draw a line to match each orb to the correct answer. One has already been done for you.

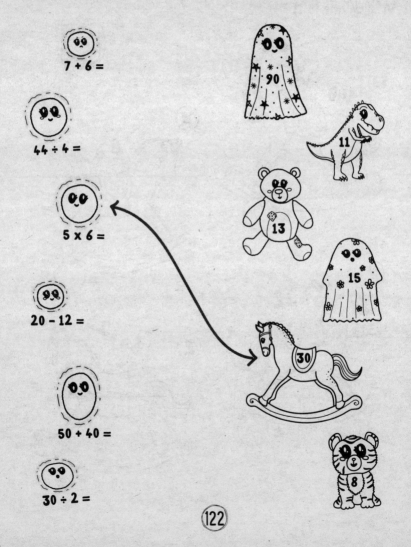

$7 + 6 =$

$44 \div 4 =$

$5 \times 6 =$

$20 - 12 =$

$50 + 40 =$

$30 \div 2 =$

90

11

13

15

30

8

Now they have their new costumes on, they can finally leave the Attic Playroom! One by one, they begin to float away...

Follow the lines and write the letter from each oval into the space at the other end of the line to reveal the words. The first letter of each word has already been done for you.

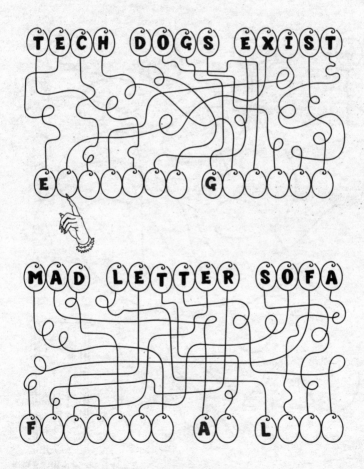

You thought the ghosts would float away through the window, never to be seen again, but they seem to be floating down through Wight Manor, all the way back to the Long Lounge... how strange!

Follow the tangled paths. Which one leads you all the way to the Long Lounge? Write your answer in the box.

Use the symbol key to crack the code and fill in the missing letters to find out what you see when you go through the door… Some letters have already been done for you.

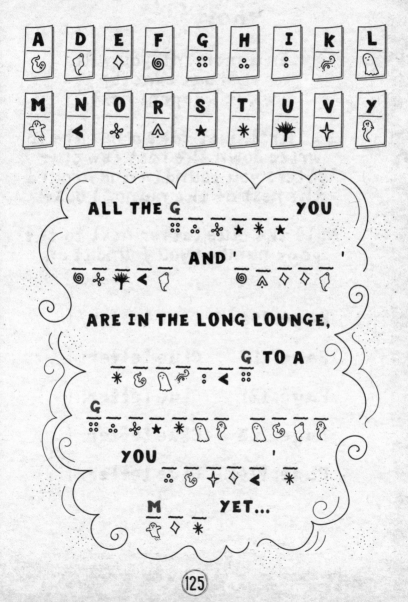

Clue Logbook:
Ghost Five

In a moment, you will
find out exactly
what happens next.

But first, just take a minute to
write down the last few clue
letters you found in and around
the rest of the manor house!

Note the clue letter next to the
page number you found it on:

Page: 106   **Clue letter:** ◯

Page: 116   **Clue letter:** ◯

Page: 121   **Clue letter:** ◯

Page: 123   **Clue letter:** ◯

Page: 124   **Clue letter:** ◯

★ The story continues... ★

They're talking to the Lady of
Wight Manor – the one who wrote the
advert in Ghost Hunter Weekly
Magazine and sent you on this ghost-
hunting quest in the first place!

And it looks like she has something
important to say to you...

Crack the code on the next page to
reveal what she says and how the
story ends.

Crack the code to finish the story!

Look back at all five Clue Logbooks
on Pages 30, 54, 78, 102 and 126.
Write the clue letters into
the key below:

(For example, because you found the letter 'R'
on Page 13, the letter 'R' is in the '13' box)

Once your key is complete, you can
crack the code to reveal the story ending!

128

"OH YES, DIDN'T YOU R_____
13 20 89 82 19 116 20

THAT I AM A G_____ T___? I'M NO
94 65 68 116 43   43 68 68

LONGER A_____, TO MY SURPRISE,
89 82 68 77 20

AND THAT'S ALL T_____ TO YOU!!!
43 65 89 77 48 116

THE S_____ YOU F_____ WERE MY
116 52 19 13 19 43 116   60 68 96 77 34

C_____ F_____. NOW FREE FROM
21 82 68 116 20 116 43   60 13 19 20 77 34 116

THEIR B_____, OUR F_____
70 68 96 77 34 116   60 13 19 20 77 34 116 65 19 52

DOESN'T HAVE TO E___. THEIR
20 77 34

B_____ YOU C_____, NOW
70 96 116 19 77 20 116 116   21 68 25 52 82 20 43 20 34

WE'RE R_____. TO THEIR
13 20 96 77 19 43 20 34

C_____ I AM T_____, WITH
21 68 25 52 89 77 106   43 13 20 89 43 20 34

YOUR WORK HERE, I'M D_____!"
34 20 82 19 94 65 43 20 34

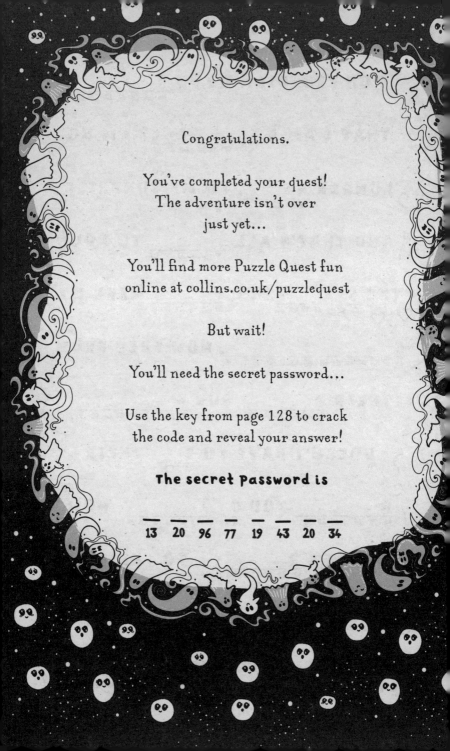

Congratulations.

You've completed your quest!
The adventure isn't over
just yet...

You'll find more Puzzle Quest fun
online at collins.co.uk/puzzlequest

But wait!

You'll need the secret password...

Use the key from page 128 to crack
the code and reveal your answer!

The secret Password is

| — | — | — | — | — | — | — | — |
| 13 | 20 | 96 | 77 | 19 | 43 | 20 | 34 |

PUZZLE
Answers

Page 10 – Silhouette Match

Page 11 – Odd One Out

Page 12 – Tangled Paths

Page 13 – Code-Cracker

THE FIRST GHOST HAUNTS THE FOREVER FOREST

A – 3
E – 6
F – 15
G – 10
H – 9
I – 25
N – 4

0 – 5
R – 2
S – 18
T – 7
U – 11
V – 13

Page 14 – Maze

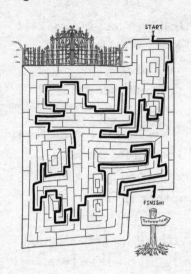

Page 15 – Order Game

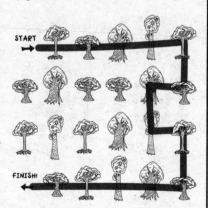

Page 16 – Sequence Puzzle

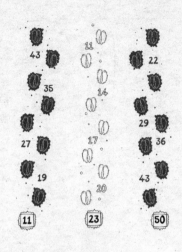

43

35

27

19

11

14

17

20

22

29

36

43

11

23

50

Page 17 – Sudoku

2	1	4	3
3	4	1	2
4	3	2	1
1	2	3	4

4	3	2	1
2	1	4	3
3	2	1	4
1	4	3	2

2	1	4	3
4	3	1	2
1	2	3	4
3	4	2	1

Page 18 – Spot the Difference

Page 20 – Word Tangle

"Of my ancestors' lockets
there are four,
I have one
but I must seek more.

In this forest I must find,
To complete my family
tree, of my own kind,
another three.

With all lockets aligned,
only then I'll be free."

Page 19 – Code-Cracker

THE
EERIE
DEERIE

Pages 21 – Odd One Out

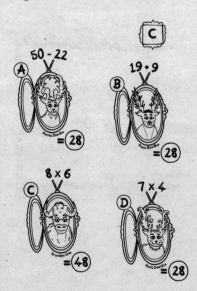

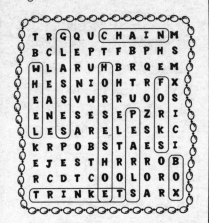

YOU FIND AUNT DEERDRIE'S LOCKET BURIED NEXT TO THE OLD STUMP.

THE ABANDONED TREEHOUSE

CONFUSED

SHOCKED

PUZZLED

PLEASE SEARCH THE REST OF THE MANOR GROUNDS FOR THE LAST LOCKET. MAYBE IF YOU FIND IT, THEN I'LL FINALLY BE FREE.

A – 6	M – 10
B – 12	N – 8
D – 2	O – 14
E – 16	R – 22
F – 20	S – 24
H – 26	T – 18
L – 4	

GREAT
UNCLE JAC

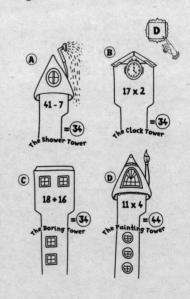

(A) The Shower Tower — 41 - 7 = 34

(B) The Clock Tower — 17 x 2 = 34

(C) The Boring Tower — 18 + 16 = 34

(D) The Painting Tower — 11 x 4 = 44

Page 35 – Maze

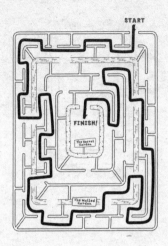

Page 37 – Tangled Paths

Page 36 – Order Game

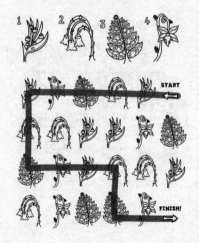

Page 38 – Sequence Puzzle

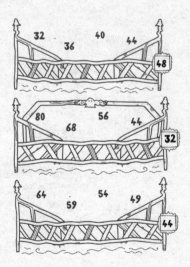

Page 39 – Sudoku

Page 41 – Odd One Out

Page 40 – Word-Wheels

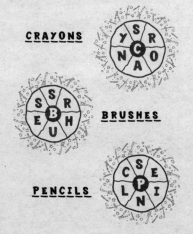

CRAYONS

BRUSHES

PENCILS

Pages 42 & 43 – Kriss Kross

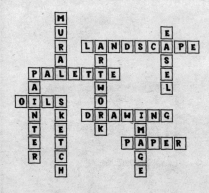

THE EASEL WEASEL

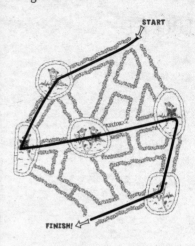

"If you're here to help me,
I'm in luck.
In this tower,
I am stuck!

In life I loved art the most,
But brushes can't be held
by a ghost.

If I am to be released,
You must complete my
masterpiece."

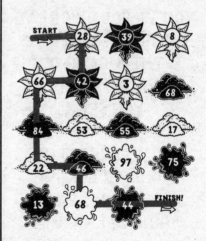

LOCKET

YOU'VE FOUND GREAT
UNCLE JAC'S LOCKET!
THE MOMENT
YOU OPEN IT,
YOU SEE A
BLUE FLASH OF
LIGHT FROM THE
FOREVER FOREST.
IT LOOKS LIKE THE
EERIE DEERIE HAS
BEEN RELEASED!

MAKE ARTS TOWER

MASTER AT WORK

EARFLAP TWIST

SELF PAWTRAIT

Page 58 – Code-Cracker

THE THIRD GHOST HAUNTS THE SHADOWY LAKE

Page 53 – Code-Cracker

I AM NO LONGER BOUND TO HAUNT THE PAINTING TOWER FOR ALL ETERNITY, YIPPEE! THANK YOU!

A – 2	P – 7
D – 6	R – 12
E – 30	T – 9
H – 11	U – 5
I – 8	W – 3
N – 15	Y – 4
O – 16	

Page 59 – Sequence Puzzle

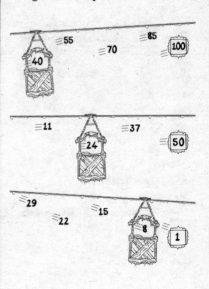

Page 60 – Word Scribble

FOLLOW THE FOUNTAINS

Page 62 – Odd One Out

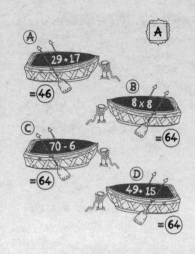

Page 61 – Order Game

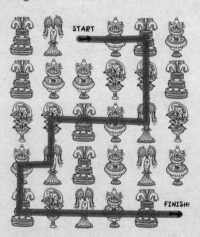

Page 63 – Maze

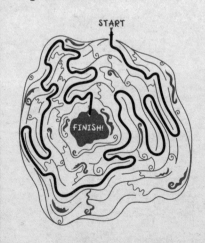

Page 64 – Code-Cracker

**BEWARE!
DEEP, DARK
AND HAUNTED
WATERS!**

Pages 66 & 67 – Wordsearch

Page 65 – Word Tangle

"You must not be here
on the lake.
You have made a big mistake!

I will haunt you
until you learn.
Don't pass the point
of no return!

If you wish to live,
Best believe, your only
option is to leave!

My ghostly voice, I know
you hear.
Go on now, get out of here!"

Page 68 – Word Tangle

Page 69 – Code-Cracker

I WORRY THAT THE LAKE
IS SO DARK IT IS TOO
DANGEROUS. I ONLY
HAUNT THE WATERS
HERE TO SCARE
PEOPLE AWAY AND
KEEP THEM SAFE!

A – 10   R – 20
D – 15   S – 45
E – 5   T – 60
H – 30   U – 65
K – 50   W – 25
N – 35   Y – 55
O – 40

Page 71 – Sudoku

1	4	3	2
3	2	1	4
2	1	4	3
4	3	2	1

4	1	2	3
2	3	4	1
1	4	3	2
3	2	1	4

2	1	3	4
4	3	1	2
3	4	2	1
1	2	4	3

Page 70 – Tangled Paths

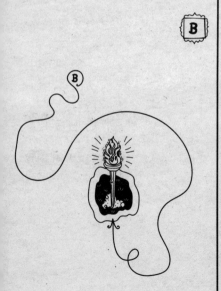

Page 72 – Order Game

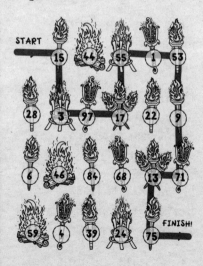

Page 73 – Maze

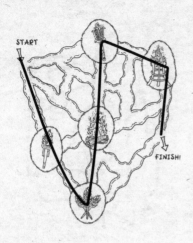

Pages 74 & 75 – Kriss Kross

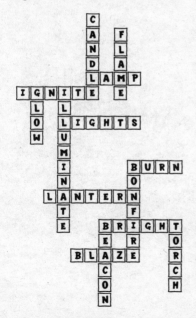

Page 76 – Word-Wheels

CALMED

HAPPY

RELAXED

Page 77 – Code-Cracker

I CAN FINALLY REST. THANK YOU FOR YOUR HELP!
HEY, I GUESS THIS MEANS WE'LL HAVE TO CHANGE MY NAME AND THE NAME OF THE LAKE! I'LL LEAVE YOU TO CHOOSE THE NEW NAMES...

Page 82 – Code-Cracker

THE FOURTH GHOST HAUNTS THE OLD CELLAR

A – 7	L – 17
C – 12	N – 5
D – 22	O – 6
E – 8	R – 27
F – 24	S – 16
G – 18	T – 4
H – 14	U – 23

Page 84 – Maze

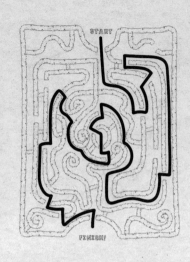

Page 83 – Sequence Puzzle

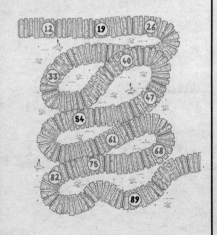

Page 85 – Spot the Difference

Page 86 – Word Tangle

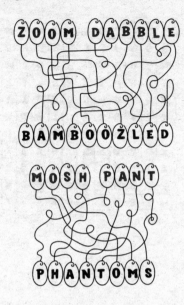

ZOOM DABBLE

BAMBOOZLED

MOSH PANT

PHANTOMS

Page 88 – Order Game

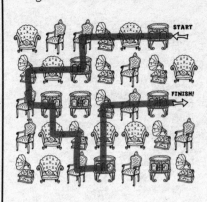

START

FINISH!

Page 87 – Maths Match

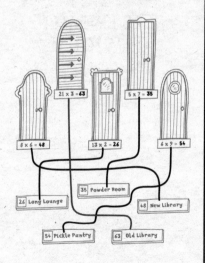

21 x 3 = **63**

5 x 7 = **35**

8 x 6 = **48**

13 x 2 = **26**

6 x 9 = **54**

26 Long Lounge

35 Powder Room

48 New Library

54 Pickle Pantry

63 Old Library

Page 89 – Odd One Out

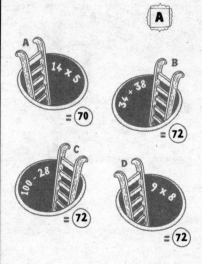

A

A 14 x 5 = 70

B 34 + 38 = 72

C 100 - 28 = 72

D 9 x 8 = 72

Pages 90 & 91 – Kriss Kross

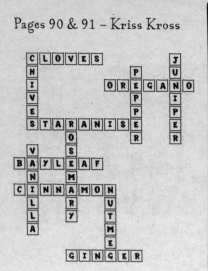

Page 92 – Order Game

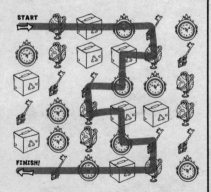

Page 93 – Wordsearch

Page 94 – Word Scribble

THE KNIGHT
OF WIGHT

Page 95 – Word Tangle

"Don't be afraid,
I am harmless,
I cry because
I'm also armless.

If you perhaps find
my missing piece,
Then my cries
would surely cease.

When you search
through the hoard
could you also try
to find my sword?"

Page 96 – Word-Wheels

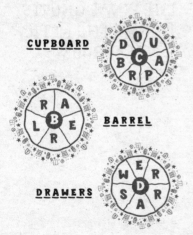

CUPBOARD

BARREL

DRAWERS

Page 97 – Missing Pieces

Page 98 – Code-Cracker

IN A SECRET ROOM
BEHIND A BOOKCASE

Page 99 – Odd One Out

Page 101 – Number Game

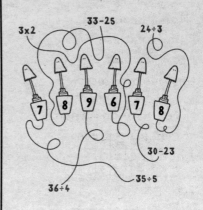

Page 100 – Code-Cracker

"QUITE SHINY
AND NEAT,
GOOD AS NEW!
I FEEL COMPLETE,
THANKS TO YOU."

A – 21	N – 5
C – 9	O – 15
D – 25	P – 18
E – 12	Q – 30
G – 7	S – 24
H – 16	T – 3
I – 6	U – 10
M – 8	

Page 106 – Code-Cracker

THE FINAL GHOSTS
HAUNT THE ATTIC
PLAYROOM

Page 107 – Sudoku

Pages 110 & 111 – Kriss Kross

Pages 108 & 109 – Wordsearch

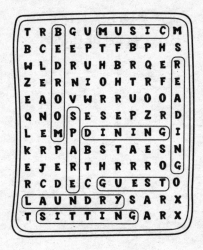

Page 112 – Order Game

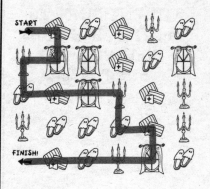

Page 113 – Spot the Difference

Page 115 – Sequence Puzzle

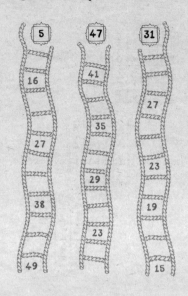

Page 114 – Code-Cracker

THE ENTRANCE TO
THE ATTIC IS HIDDEN
BEHIND THE
FIREPLACE

Page 116 – Word Scribble

"WE ARE
THE ORBS"

Page 117 – Word Tangle

"We are ghosts with no shell,
Things to haunt would be swell.
Some of us want sheets,
That would be really sweet.
For some, to become a toy
Would bring so much joy.
To have a disguise
Would be the true prize.
Can you find us somewhere to hide?
We'd be grateful if you tried!"

Page 119 – Odd One Out

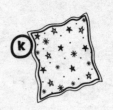

Page 118 – Silhouette Match

Page 120 – Order Game

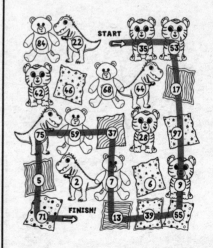

Page 121 – Odd One Out

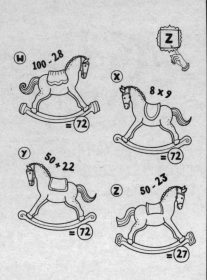

W. $100 - 28$ = 72

X. 8×9 = 72

Y. $50 + 22$ = 72

Z. $50 - 23$ = 27

Page 122 – Maths Match

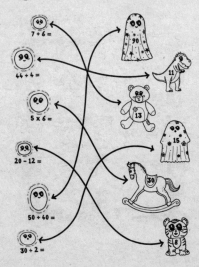

$7 + 6 =$

$44 \div 4 =$

$5 \times 6 =$

$20 - 12 =$

$50 + 40 =$

$30 \div 2 =$

90

11

13

15

30

8

Page 123 – Word Tangle

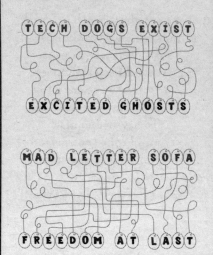

TECH DOGS EXIST

EXCITED GHOSTS

MAD LETTER SOFA

FREEDOM AT LAST

Page 124 – Tangled Paths

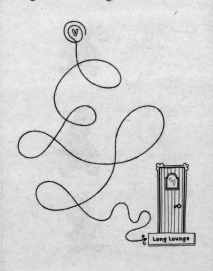

V

Long Lounge

ALL THE GHOSTS YOU
FOUND AND 'FREED'
ARE IN THE LONG
LOUNGE,
TALKING TO A
GHOSTLY LADY
YOU HAVEN'T
MET YET...

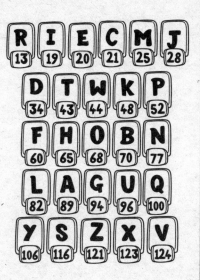

"OH YES, DIDN'T
YOU REALISE
THAT I AM A
GHOST TOO?
I'M NO LONGER ALONE,
TO MY SURPRISE,
AND THAT'S ALL
THANKS TO YOU!
THE SPIRITS YOU
FOUND WERE MY
CLOSEST FRIENDS.
NOW FREE FROM
THEIR BOUNDS,
OUR FRIENDSHIP
DOESN'T HAVE TO END.
THEIR BUSINESS
YOU COMPLETED, NOW
WE'RE REUNITED.
TO THEIR
COMPANY I AM TREATED.
WITH YOUR WORK HERE,
I'M DELIGHTED!"

✴ Notes ✴

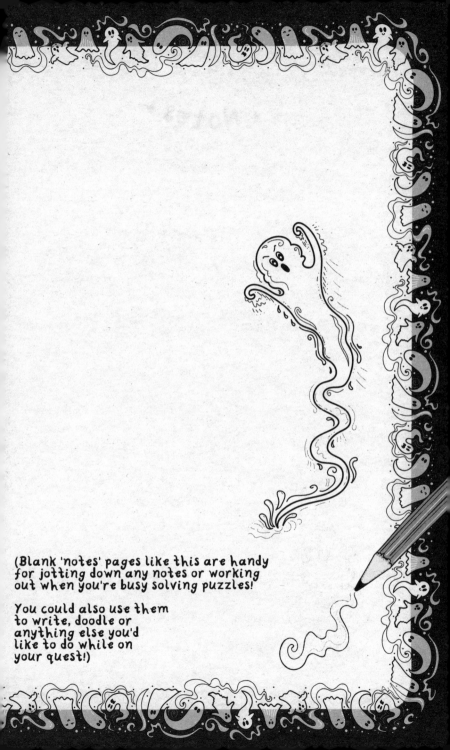

(Blank 'notes' pages like this are handy
for jotting down any notes or working
out when you're busy solving puzzles!

You could also use them
to write, doodle or
anything else you'd
like to do while on
your quest!)

★ Notes ★

✷ Notes ✷